THE PREGNANCY PROPOSITION

BY
MEREDITH WEBBER

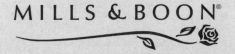

'I've tried to think of ways to say it that don't sound bad, but I can't.

'The thing is, Peterson, since that night—you know the one I mean—well, I can't help thinking how good things were between us, and I wondered if you felt the same and how you'd feel about regular contacts like it.'

Amelia frowned at him as she tried to make sense of this garbled sentence.

'"Regular contacts"?' she repeated faintly. 'Are you suggesting we start going out together?'

'Good heavens, no,' Mac said, promptly. 'Not a relationship. I'm no good at relationships, I told you that. But getting together every now and then…'

'Physically? As in sex? You're suggesting you pop over to _____ ___ ____ for a quick—'

'No, no, no_ ___ ____ _____ _____ ____joyed the dinner, t___ _____ _____ _____ dinner as well…'

First published in Great Britain 2003
Harlequin Mills & Boon Limited,
Eton House, 18-24 Paradise Road, Richmond, Surrey TW9 1SR

© Meredith Webber 2003

ISBN 0 263 83460 3

Set in Times Roman 10½ on 12 pt.
03-0803-47472

Printed and bound in Spain
by Litografia Rosés, S.A., Barcelona

CHAPTER ONE

FRASER MCDOUGAL, known to friends, staff and those patients of St Patrick's Hospital conscious or lucid enough to remember his casually informal introduction as Mac, sat in the small partitioned-off space laughingly called an office and wondered what the treatment was for a doctor drowned in paperwork.

A frustrated, headachy doctor drowned in paperwork.

'On autopsy, would they find masses of shredded paper blocking my lungs?' he mused, frowning at the untidy piles as if his disapproval might magically make them disappear. 'Paper petechiae in my eyes?'

'Talking to yourself, Mac?'

He looked up and smiled.

For some reason, most people smiled at Peterson. It wasn't that she was wildly attractive. In fact, she was quite ordinary-looking if you considered her bit by bit—short in stature, body slim as a boy's, brown hair ruthlessly hauled back into some kind of bunched arrangement at the back, though after even an hour at work, bits of it stuck out every which way on her head—but she had good bones and the kind of mobile face one knew instinctively would smile easily.

'No more than usual,' he replied. 'But if you've come to tell me I'm needed out there, forget it. I've been officially off duty for two hours, and even in Accident and Emergency I think I'm entitled to a break.'

'If you want a break, you have to leave the hospital—you should know that by now.' Without waiting for an

5

invitation, Peterson cleared a pile of papers off the spare chair and plonked herself down on it. 'Anyway, I don't want you to see a patient. I want to ask a favour.'

Mac frowned. He had no idea what Peterson's favour might be, but he hated being put in situations where he had to say no. Best he get in early.

'If it's to partner you to the hospital dance, then no. You know I don't do that stuff. And if it's to—'

'Hospital dance? What hospital dance?'

Mac felt his frown grow deeper—just what he needed, ploughed-field-furrow-type wrinkles!

'Isn't there always a hospital dance?'

Peterson shrugged.

'Not that I know of, but, believe me, Mac, I'd as soon ask the lad who delivers gorilla-grams as ask you to a dance. Though, if he wore his gorilla suit, people might think I was with you.'

Mac's facial expressions shifted from frown to scowl. There'd been some ridiculous movie a few years ago in which, as far as he could make out, an idiot man who thought he was a gorilla was rescued by an unlikely blonde and brought to the big city. Most of the staff had decided Mac could have been his double, and gorilla jokes had raged around the department for weeks. And all because he rarely had time for a haircut, and looked more unshaven than most other male doctors after a twelve-hour stint in A and E.

'Hardly a diplomatic remark, Peterson, when you're here to ask a favour!'

'I know,' she said penitently, though the sparkle dancing in her brown eyes belied the contrite look on her face.

But still she hesitated, and Mac, feeling more and more certain it was something he definitely didn't want to do, decided he'd better take the initiative. Again!

'Well, whatever it is, don't bother,' he growled at her. 'I'm rarely in the mood to do favours for anyone, and right now I'm even less compliant—or complacent, come to that. Can't you see this paperwork? Can't you see I'm under siege here? And the department's as short-staffed as ever, so taking time to do it during working hours just isn't an option. The paperwork, not whatever favour you want.'

Peterson returned his scowl with one of her own.

'Oh, spare me!' she said. 'I could practically recite your complaints, I've heard them all so often. If you didn't think you had to see, personally, every drifter who wanders through our doors, and if you didn't feel you had to check on the work of every medical officer under you, and most of the nursing staff as well, you'd have plenty of time to do your paperwork during your shift.'

Incensed by this unjust criticism, Mac scowled harder.

'You know how many of the medical staff we get lumbered with couldn't give a damn about A and E patients. They consider their time here a necessary evil in their intern year and treat the patients like objects on a conveyor belt,' he reminded her. 'And some of those drifters just might be hatching something deadly so, of course, I like to keep my finger on the pulse of things.'

'A finger's OK,' his visitor retorted, 'but you give the whole hand, and all the rest of yourself. You've no idea of delegation—'

Mac held up his hand to halt the flow, and Peterson grinned at him.

'OK,' she conceded. 'You can recite off my complaints as word perfect as I can spout yours. Quits?'

Mac nodded and, forgetting she'd come in for a reason as yet undivulged, pulled a tray of papers towards him.

Amelia Peterson sighed.

She'd dropped in to ask a simple favour and somehow they'd got sidetracked. Now the wretched man had forgotten she was there.

'Mac!'

He glanced up, and the face that would have been handsome if it hadn't been almost permanently etched with tiredness took on a puzzled expression.

'The favour,' she said patiently.

Mac's hazel eyes with their heavy lids and dark rich fringe of lashes peered suspiciously at her.

'Haven't you already asked? Didn't I say no?'

'You said no to a hospital dance!' she said crossly. 'As *if*!'

If he hadn't been six-two to her midget dimensions of five-three, she'd have shaken him. Instead she sighed.

'The favour I want is simple enough. You're on the medical advisory committee, aren't you?'

'The other MAC? Yes, for my sins. I can't imagine why they wanted me on it—and a bigger waste of time I've never known. I mean, I know it's necessary to have one and there are—'

But Amelia wasn't going to let him get sidetracked again.

'Don't start!' she warned, holding up her hand to emphasise the warning. 'Just listen! I want to set up a structured in-service training process here for the A and E nurses, but it would need the approval of the director of nursing—'

'Well, I'm sure I'd be influential there!' Mac said dryly. 'She doesn't attend all the MAC meetings but even if she did, I doubt we've ever met without having a difference of opinion about something.'

'She's not that bad,' Amelia protested. 'You just don't like women.'

'Me not like women?' He overdid the reaction. 'Of course I like women. I was even married to one once!'

Sidetracked again, Amelia rolled her eyes.

'Forget the DON, forget your ex-wife, forget *all* women, and just listen,' she said sternly. 'At the moment—well, almost always, in fact—the majority of the A and E nurses are older, and have worked in every other hospital department before coming here. They need that experience to be able to make the quick assessments necessary down here. But spending ten years in A and E doesn't necessarily make you better at the job, whereas a structured programme of in-service training would enhance professionalism and give emergency nurses the opportunity to pursue a distinct clinical career.'

The heavy lids lifted so the hazel eyes could look more closely at her.

'You sound as if you're reciting something you read in a textbook. Tell me what good would it do. How it would improve nursing services in this department.'

Determined not to sigh again, Amelia closed her eyes—briefly—and took a deep breath.

'Let's take communication skills as an example,' she began. 'With conscious patients, assessment begins with communication—establishing a dialogue with the patient. Shirley Cribb is probably one of the most experienced nurses in the department and certainly one of the best at inserting an IV catheter. But any patient unlucky enough to strike her for initial assessment would wonder why he'd bothered to come to hospital.'

Mac actually smiled.

'And what's wrong with you?' he growled, imitating Shirley's gruff voice to perfection. 'Don't you have a GP you could have seen rather than wasting our time down here?'

'Exactly,' Amelia said. 'And though we all try to encourage casual attendees to use their own GPs—or a twenty-four-hour clinic—rather than the hospital, that's not the way to do it.'

'And you think sending Shirley on a communication course would help? Would she go?'

'Probably not voluntarily,' Amelia admitted. 'In fact, the courses are already offered by the hospital's professional development team, and Shirley certainly hasn't taken advantage of the offer up to now, but if it was part of a structured in-service training programme, then she'd have to go.'

'I can see that,' Mac agreed, 'but what's it got to do with me? You're the senior A and E nurse. You can do what you like with your staff, arrange whatever programmes you want, can't you?'

This time Amelia's sigh escaped. She might have known this would be his reaction. If Mac wanted something done he just did it and worried about the consequences later. Which was OK for a medical head of department, but not quite so OK for a nurse—however senior she might be.

She shook her head. There were days when she was just too tired to talk to Mac, but this was too important to let slide.

'To a certain extent—yes! But with a programme like this—there are courses in bereavement counselling, in paramedical emergencies, in respiratory therapy, so many things that are relevant to an A and E nurse—you need to have the in-service training as a policy so staff can be allocated paid leave to attend the courses, and the rosters altered so the department isn't left short-staffed.'

'Ha! Money! It'll never happen. You know how tight

the budget is, and you're suggesting *I* suggest they spend more. Nice one, Peterson!'

'I'm not suggesting anything of the kind,' Amelia said crossly. 'In-service training is supposed to be compulsory in all workplaces, and it's in place in the hospital, so there's already a budget for it. But there are no A-and-E-specific courses, so the nursing staff down here ignore the other courses which could be beneficial to them, and no one follows up to see whether they're complying with the overall hospital policy.'

'So, how do you get around that? If the courses are already there and no one wants to take them, how do you make people trot along?'

He was worse than a two-year-old with his questions!

Praying for patience, she sorted through her thoughts, still anxious, in spite of his lack of interest, to win his support.

'By structuring them into an incentive programme. In the US, there's been an enormous rise in the number of nurse-practitioners, nurses who are able to take more responsibility than regular RNs. And the first of these nurse-practitioners has recently been appointed in New South Wales. They can give drugs without a doctor's permission, and initiate treatment—'

'And your nurses would take on those roles?' Disbelief reverberated in his voice.

'No, but they'd be on their way to that position should it be introduced here. It makes sense, Mac, because it would free up doctors for more important matters and be a great financial saving throughout the hospital. And the nurses would achieve seniority, and subsequent pay rises, through training, rather than the length of service—or as well as length of service.'

'I still don't see where I come into it,' Mac told her. 'It's really got nothing to do with me.'

'Having more efficient nurses in A and E is nothing to do with you? I'd have thought it had a great deal to do with you!'

Unable to deny this point, he made do with frowning at her. 'I'd have thought hands-on experience in A and E would be worth a thousand courses. Look at you. How long have you been here? Were you here when I arrived? I seem to remember a little bit of a thing scurrying around the place. Thought we had mice!'

She picked up a medical journal and threw it at him.

'I've already done a range of extra courses and, yes, I think it makes me a better nurse. It's made me see the job as more than a station on a conveyor belt, where people come in and are either shunted out or shunted up to somewhere else. It helps me remember that each patient is an individual, and that the process of nursing involves treating him or her as such.'

She held up her hand to stop him interrupting again.

'I know that kind of thing is written in stone in all the hospital aims and objectives and in its mission statement, but in A and E it's easy to use the excuse of being busy and to duck a lot of the issues involved in measuring up to the highest possible standards.'

Tired though he was, Mac still had the urge to smile at Peterson's enthusiasm. She was like that whatever she did—whether organising to get the waiting room redecorated or selling raffle tickets for some obscure fundraising appeal—she threw herself whole-heartedly into it.

But he wasn't going to be inveigled into more effort by Peterson's enthusiasm.

'I still don't see where I come into it,' he told her,

hoping she'd finally get the message that he wasn't going to get involved. 'It's a nursing problem.'

'Not if you see A and E as an integrated service,' she snapped, glaring at him, though her eyes glinted as if she knew she'd won the point. 'Which,' she added in softer, almost dulcet tones, 'you are always telling us it is.'

'Smug doesn't suit you!' Knowing he was trapped, he glared right back at her. 'So forget all the flowery stuff about mission statements and tell me what you think I could possibly do about this great idea.'

'You could bring it up at a MAC meeting, and then it would be tabled, and next time I talk to the DON, she can't mouth placating phrases and do absolutely nothing.'

'You mean you've already spoken to her about this?' Mac demanded. 'And you expect me to air it again?' He knew he sounded incredulous, but the word didn't begin to describe his disbelief. 'To Enid Biggs? That woman already hates my guts. We argue every time she's present at a meeting. She—'

'She won't be there.' Peterson interrupted him before he could get into full flow on the problems he'd had with the DON. 'She's off at a conference for like-minded autocrats. Won't be back for a fortnight.'

Peterson's finely boned face looked momentarily remorseful.

'That was mean!' she said quickly. 'She does a good job, and most Directors of Nursing were excellent nurses before they went into management, but it's because she won't be here that I thought now was the time to get it tabled.'

'Sneak it in under her guard? Couldn't that bounce back on you?'

Peterson's elfin face lit up as she smiled with mischievous delight.

'On me? *I* didn't bring it up.'

Mac shook his head.

'Look, I'd like to help out, but I know damn well what something like that would mean. First they'll want an analysis of the current system—'

'There isn't one!'

He ignored Peterson's interruption and continued, 'And evaluations of this, comparisons of that and more paperwork to add to the conglomeration of bumf already accumulated in my office.'

He frowned severely at her, partly because he wanted her to understand no meant no but also because he felt slightly bad about not helping.

'And don't bother telling me that I won't be affected by any change. I spent years convincing the hospital it needed a specialist director of A and E, and when they finally decided I might be right and appointed me, they realised they had somewhere to dump all the stuff other people didn't want to do. I'm supposed to spend half my life evaluating and analysing and comparing one system with another and I just don't have the time. So, no, Peterson, count me out.'

Amelia clamped her lips tightly shut so the things she'd have liked to yell at him didn't escape. Instead she stood up, gave him one final black look and flung open the door.

Which was when her control broke.

'Thanks for nothing!' she snapped. 'And don't bother asking for my help next time you have an emergency intubation or a cardiac arrest because I'll be too busy organising staff schedules and doing my own paperwork.'

She slammed the door behind her and stormed down the corridor, heading for her locker, where she retrieved her handbag, but was still too furious to realise she should also have grabbed her jacket. It might be nearly spring in Southern Queensland, but the evenings were still chilly.

Mac watched the door reverberate, and dismissed the faint twinge of regret down deep where his conscience used to be. He assured himself he'd made the right decision, but he felt bad about disappointing Peterson. She was the finest A and E nurse he'd come across. Not that she'd carry out her threat of not assisting him when he needed it. She was far too dedicated to not help where she was needed.

Wasn't she?

The phone rang before he had time to answer his own question.

He hated the phone almost as much as he hated paperwork.

'Mac!' he bellowed into the receiver—knowing such an intimidatory tactic could make wimpy callers hang up.

'Your phone-answering skills haven't improved.'

Cool amusement in a so-familiar voice!

'Helene?'

'How are you, Mac?'

'I'm sure you're not phoning to enquire about my health,' he told her bluntly, knowing his frown lines were growing deeper by the millisecond, though his ex-wife was close to two thousand kilometres away.

'No, I'm not. You haven't returned your A4726.'

Mac took a very deep breath, but that didn't stop the explosion.

'Like hell!' he bellowed into the inoffensive instrument now clutched in a white-knuckled hand. 'I haven't a clue what your A-whatever is when it's at home, but I do know that Ms Running-the-Federal-Health-Department Clinton sure as hell isn't in charge of collecting them. You must have dozens of minions—hundreds most likely—doing those little menial tasks for you.'

'The A4726 is part of an Australia-wide survey of A and E Departments, designed for analysis and evaluation of resources available to patient-specific sectors of the community.'

Mac rubbed his pounding temple. 'Please, tell me you didn't just say that, Helene?' he begged. 'Please, tell me I couldn't have married someone capable of such painfully bureaucratic mumbo-jumbo?'

'Don't play games, Mac,' Helene said crisply. 'I've been at parties where you've bored people rigid with medical jargon. You could bore for Australia on emergency medicine. Anyway, I would have thought filling in the A4726 would have been to your distinct advantage.'

Helene suggesting something to his advantage?

The same Helene who'd left him stuck in a dingy townhouse they'd once bought as an investment because she'd had the nous to hire a divorce lawyer while he'd had some ludicrous idea they could discuss the distribution of their assets like adults?

Adults! Ha! Even a child could divide by two.

'Well?'

The demand made him shake his head in an effort to get back to the present. The movement reminded him of the headache.

'Well, what?' he said stupidly, thinking headache relief not paperwork, and using his free hand to rummage through the mess on his desk in search of a blister pack of paracetamol he knew he had somewhere.

'Well, didn't you realise when you read it just how advantageous it could be to you? As the only specialist A and E director in Lakelands, a rationalisation of the A and E departments in the city would be to your advantage. St Pat's would be sure to get the nod as the main trauma centre, and you'd get funding for extra staff and equipment, plus a bigger annual budget. And I'm just talking Federal funds. Because health is primarily a state concern, the State would come to the party as well. They're finally seeing the wisdom of rationalisation.'

Mac put his hand across his forehead and tried squeezing his temples, but that didn't help either the headache or his understanding.

'Maybe Colleen—' he began, but Helene cut him short.

'Don't blame your secretary because you're hopeless at paperwork. Honestly, Mac, I thought you might have grown up by now. At least matured enough to realise that the record-keeping you so despise is just as important as the patients you treat.'

He shook his head in disbelief, not so much that anyone could actually think such a thing but that he'd once been in love with someone—a fellow doctor at that—who held so divergent a view of medicine. The head-shaking didn't help the headache and his searching fingers were yet to find a packet of paracetamol among the debris on his desk.

'I'll find the form, I'll fill it in,' he promised, willing to do anything to get Helene off the phone.

'Oh, I'm not ringing about that,' she said cheerfully. 'Although the sooner you get it in the better. I'm ringing to say I'll be in Lakelands for a couple of days. We've built a conceptual representation of the situation but need to do some on-site work, and we'll be starting there.'

'Conceptual representation?' Mac repeated helplessly. He'd found the blister pack but, of course, his coffee-cup was completely empty and there was no other fluid within reach. 'What the hell are you talking about now?'

Maybe he could chew the tablets and swallow them dry. He'd probably choke to death...

'Don't pull the dumb act on me, Mac,' Helene said. 'Not that it matters whether you understand or not. I'll be up there and I thought we might get together. I'd really like to, actually. There's someone I want you to meet.'

Mac felt his gut tighten. He and Helene had been separated for five years and divorced for three, and the strongest emotion he'd felt at any stage had been relief. Now apprehension was creeping in, and a whole lot of doubt.

'Why?'

'Because it's important to me,' she said, then she added the clincher. 'Please, Mac?'

It had taken a while but he'd finally trained himself to say no to any requests that didn't ultimately help his work or, on increasingly rare occasions, provide pleasure in his life. Hadn't he just managed it with Peterson?

But before he could utter the simple syllable, Helene said 'please' again, and he found 'Well, if you must!' coming out instead.

'Great,' she purred. 'We'll be arriving in town Saturday morning. I'll get my secretary to book at Capriccio's. Eight suit you?'

Still recovering from his capitulation, he must have made a garbled noise which Helene took for agreement. Or perhaps she'd simply assumed he'd agree—taken his compliance for granted.

'Shall I make it for four?'

Four?

Mac lifted the receiver away from his ear and frowned at it, before returning it to position to say, 'I thought you said eight?'

Low musical laughter.

'Table for four, you dolt! Surely you're seeing someone by now?'

'Seeing someone? Oh! Yes. Of course. Eight at Capriccio's.'

Mac hung up, then stared blankly into space. Actually he stared blankly ahead, which meant he saw more of his office door than the space.

Office door.

Slamming shut…

Peterson.

He shot out of his chair, crossed the room in two strides, flung open the door and launched himself down the corridor, bellowing 'Peterson!' as he went.

'She's gone!' One of the scrub-clad figures hurrying in the other direction pointed towards the staff exit. 'I saw her shoot through there about five minutes ago.'

Mac followed, hoping he might catch her in the car park. If she had a car… He frowned into the light-brightened area, trying to remember if he'd ever seen Peterson parking a car here—driving a car.

Of course she had a car. Hadn't he driven her home a couple of times when they'd had a late meeting and it had been being serviced?

The blare of a horn and headlights striking him simultaneously reminded him of where he was, and he stepped back between a row of parked cars. The approaching vehicle stopped, and a familiar head poked out the driver's window.

'Feeling so guilty about saying no you're trying to commit suicide, Mac?'

'Peterson!' He greeted the taunting voice with relief. 'I was looking for you. I wanted to tell you I'd changed my mind.'

The place was well lit enough for him to see the shifts in her expression. Disbelief, fleeting pleasure, then suspicion—the changes as rapid as eye blinks.

'Why?'

'So you'd know, of course. The next meeting isn't until next week, but I'll bring it up. In the meantime, if we could get together so you can explain it more fully...'

She was frowning now, and the suspicious look had become more marked. Nobody's fool, Peterson.

'I meant why did you change your mind, not why were you looking for me,' she said gruffly.

'Actually, Peterson, it's a quid pro quo thing. I've a favour to ask of you.'

Ignoring the fact that her car—one of those midget four-wheel-drive vehicles that were proliferating on the roads these days—was blocking the exit lane, she turned off the engine and opened the door, leaping out to land in front of him.

'You've a favour to ask of me?' she repeated, totally overdoing the incredulity. 'And if I say yes, you'll raise the primary nursing issue with the MAC?'

Mac nodded, although, now she'd put it so bluntly, he was beginning to feel a little uncomfortable.

'It's a legitimate trade,' he stressed, looking down into her face which with the play of light and shadow had taken on an even more elfin look—all cheekbones and wide eyes, narrowing to a sultry mouth and pointed chin. 'Favour for a favour.'

The suspicion didn't shift.

'My favour is for the good of the department,' she said, wrapping her arms around her shoulders as if she was cold. 'Not even so much a favour as a simple, work-related request.'

'Yes, well, mine is too,' Mac hastened to assure her, remembering Helene saying something about how filling out some blasted form would be to St Pat's benefit.

Amelia rubbed warmth into her arms and looked up at

him. Every instinct in her body was telling her to walk away—actually, she'd get back into her car and drive away, but walk away was how her nerves were putting it.

But setting up the in-service training process in A and E was important to her, and what could Mac possibly ask that would be so distasteful she'd rather lose his co-operation than say yes?

'What's the favour?'

'You don't have to sound so suspicious,' he grumbled. 'It's perfectly simple. All I want you to do is have dinner with me on Saturday night.'

'Have dinner with you on Saturday night? As in a date, Mac?'

He glared at her.

'Of course it's not a date. Just dinner.'

'With you?'

She was aware she must sound half-witted, but it was like some huge mathematical puzzle so involved her brain refused to process even the simple bits of information.

'With me,' he confirmed. 'Capriccio's at eight. OK?'

This, too, was bizarre enough to bear repeating, but she had a feeling she'd been repeating things since the strange conversation had begun so made a conscious effort not to do it again. She looked up into his face, wishing she could read the expression in his usually expressive eyes, but with the light behind him his face was nothing more than a dark blur.

'And if I do this, you'll bring up the primary nursing process at the next MAC meeting?'

He nodded.

'You promise?'

'Oh, for Pete's sake, Peterson, what do you want? A neon sign? An oath signed in blood? I've said I'll do it and I will. Have you something to wear?'

It was all too much for Amelia. She felt the tickle of a giggle start deep inside her, but she held back the laughter that wanted to follow.

'No, Mac, I'll come naked,' she said, allowing a chuckle to escape as she shook her head at him. 'Honestly!'

She was still laughing as she climbed back into her car, started the engine, tooted the horn at him, still standing between two parked cars, and drove off into the night.

CHAPTER TWO

THOUGH Amelia had continued chuckling all the way home—the thought of Mac being driven to bargain for a date was hilarious—by the time she reported to work the next morning, she was more apprehensive than amused.

What was on at Capriccio's that Mac needed a date?

And where were all the women he was supposed to have on a string? Back when his marriage had broken up, rumour had had it he'd been at fault, and though Amelia had never seen him out with anyone, or known of anyone in the hospital dating him, she was reasonably certain an attractive and obviously virile man like Mac would have women falling over themselves to go out with him.

'Ha! You're here. I need you in cubicle four. There's a cardiac arrest in three. We've stabilised him but now the wife's collapsed. I want the crash team to stay with the man until we're sure he won't arrest again. You check out the woman.'

Amelia accepted Mac's orders with equanimity, even relief, for this was the Mac she knew, prowling A and E, taking charge of difficult cases, giving orders right, left and centre. From the way he sounded, he certainly hadn't been harbouring any hidden desire for her which had suddenly resulted in the previous evening's invitation.

She walked into cubicle four, where a woman was being lifted onto a trolley.

'Put her on her side,' she told the orderlies, moving closer so she could angle the woman's head to clear her airway. At the same time, her mind ranged through pos-

23

sible causes for the collapse, the most likely being delayed shock. While her husband had needed her she'd managed to keep going, but once assured he was receiving the best professional attention she'd relaxed. Just a little too much.

Amelia began her visual assessment, at the same time attaching a cardio-respiratory and pulse oximeter monitor.

'I'll take blood—the doctor will want to check, particularly the blood-sugar level,' she told the junior who'd arrived to assist.

The woman stirred, then opened her eyes.

Amelia saw the panic in them even before the patient tried to sit up.

'I'm not sick, it's my husband. He had a heart attack. Where is he? Why am I here?'

Amelia explained, reassuring the woman her husband was receiving the very best of care in the cubicle next door. Then she began the routine questioning of the patient, writing details on a new admittance form, knowing a lot more would be added before the patient—Mrs Creed—went home.

Rick Stewart, the A and E registrar on duty, came in, and Amelia handed him the form, then excused herself as she was paged to report to Triage.

Sally Spender, the triage nurse on duty, was surrounded by a group of wailing, shouting people, several of them holding children. The women's head coverings as well as their dark beauty, suggested they belonged to the large Muslim population in the suburbs surrounding the hospital.

'Looks like food poisoning,' Sally said, pushing her way through the group towards Amelia. 'Can you give me a hand sorting the sick from the panickers?'

Amelia chose the tallest man in the group.

'Can you speak English?' she asked him, and he nodded.

'And the rest of them? If I speak to them in English, will they understand?'

'Some will, but not the women. Not all the women.' He corrected himself carefully.

'Then could you, please, ask them all to sit down? I will see each of them in turn and start treatment, then the doctor will see those who are the sickest first. OK?'

The man nodded, and turned towards the crowd, speaking to them in a language that sounded strangely musical to Amelia.

Whatever he said, it worked, for the group shuffled towards vacant chairs and, one by one, sat. Sally whipped down the line, handing out kidney dishes in case anyone needed one, while Amelia waited until she was done before speaking to the man, who introduced himself as Taraq, again.

'Will you come with me in case I need someone to translate? The hospital has a translator but it will take time to page her and get her down here so it's quicker this way.'

She moved towards the group as she spoke, visually assessing them, choosing first a woman with a small child of about two cradled in her arms.

'Can you tell me what happened?' she asked Taraq, as she checked the child's pulse.

'We have a special day today, and after morning prayers a special feast. Not a lot of food, just rice cakes and sweetmeats. Then, so soon, people began to feel sick.'

'Pre-cooked rice can harbour nasty bacteria,' Amelia told him, knowing the incident would have to be reported and any leftover food tested.

'Or the sweetmeats,' Taraq said. 'We have brought samples as we know you will need these.'

He pointed to a number of foil-wrapped parcels on the reception desk.

'Very good thinking,' Amelia told him, bending to speak to an elderly woman who was doubled over with pain. 'Now, if you could tell this lady I want to take her to a treatment room…'

Taraq translated, and though Amelia tried to help, a younger man set her firmly aside, saying, 'I will take her and wait with her, speak for her.'

'That is her grandson,' her translator explained. 'She adheres to the old ways. It would not be right for her to be seen by a doctor without a male of her family present.'

'Fair enough,' Amelia said, directing another patient, a young toddler accompanied by his father, to another treatment room.

She then paused and took stock. She knew no patient should leave A and E without being seen by a doctor, but some of these people were more scared than ill. They were also, as far as triage—the system of sorting the most ill from the least ill—was concerned, way down the list as far as priority for seeing a doctor went. Which meant they might be waiting for a long time, and from previous experience she knew this could sometimes be construed as racial bias.

Tread carefully, she warned herself, before turning back to the man she'd appointed as her helper.

'Now, if you could explain to them all that, although they are feeling bad right now, we cannot give them anything that will make them feel better immediately.'

Taraq, who until then had been treating her with some respect, gave her a look of total disbelief.

'But you are hospital!' he said.

'Yes, I know,' Amelia explained. 'But here's what happens. Although we won't know for sure what bacteria caused the illness until the food is tested, we can narrow it down to a couple of possibilities because these people felt sick so soon after eating. The names won't mean much to you, but I'd say it was either *Staphylococcus aureus* or *Bacillus cercus.* Other bacterial sicknesses take longer to show up, something in the region of twelve to thirty-six hours.'

Taraq nodded, but was still looking unhappily at his compatriots who sat in a miserable line on the waiting room chairs.

'Now, though the symptoms these people are experiencing are unpleasant, they aren't life-threatening. Very young people and very old people are more at risk because of dehydration, which can affect the body's functioning, but we'll do something about that. With this type of food poisoning, it's better to let it work its way out of the system. If we give patients drugs to stop them vomiting, it also stops the toxin's progress through the body so, unless vomiting is very severe, we don't treat it.'

She looked hopefully at Taraq.

'Do you understand all that?'

He nodded again, though he obviously wasn't happy.

'They must stay sick?'

'For a little while,' Amelia said. 'Though we'll do something to stop it if the vomiting becomes severe. In the meantime, I can organise special drinks for all those who've been sick, to help rehydrate them and restore the balance of the various chemicals in their bodies.'

He seemed more pleased now, so Amelia decided she'd better get to the bit she didn't particularly want to mention, but knew she had to if she wanted to avoid any issues of bias in the treatment of the group.

'The main problem is, they should all stay until they've seen a doctor, but, because they aren't emergency cases, other people might be called to see a doctor sooner than your friends will, although they have been here longer. We work on the severity of the case, rather than first come first served. Do you understand that?'

The frown became a scowl, but at that moment a doctor was paged and asked to go to treatment room three, the one the old lady occupied, and Amelia seized the initiative.

'You see, she will be seen right now, because of the risk for older people, and the children will be seen next, as soon as there's a doctor available. It is only those less ill who might have to wait.'

At that moment, the wide doors wheezed open and a young man entered, his left hand supporting his right arm just above the wrist. Blood was pouring from a wound at the base of his thumb and splashing onto the floor.

'I see now. It is right you fix that young man first. I will explain this.'

Sally was already with the young man, wrapping a towel around his hand, hustling him towards a cubicle. Amelia followed her, sighing with relief.

She wouldn't have wished such a bad wound on anyone, but seeing the young man come in had made it clear to the group with sick stomachs why the doctors saw people on the basis of need.

The day proceeded as it had begun, patients pouring in through the doors, as if they'd been holding off all their ailments for just such an occasion. Altogether, eighteen people from the breakfast feast were treated, but as each sick person had been accompanied by anything from one to six relatives, the waiting room had seemed full to capacity all day.

At six, an hour and a half after she was due off duty, but satisfied things had finally returned to normal, Amelia made her escape, heading first for the tearoom where the nurses had their lockers.

She'd caught fleeting glimpses of Mac during the day, but had had no time to talk to him about anything other than the state of play in the department. Neither had she had time to think about their bargain, apart from a moment when she'd replayed the previous evening's conversation and had felt annoyed that he'd obviously assumed she wouldn't already have a date on a Saturday night.

Or a man in her life who might object to her going out with someone else, even for a business-related evening!

Though, apart from the rotating interns, student nurses and junior residents, most of the A and E staff were permanent fixtures so they all knew each other reasonably well. She rarely gossiped, and had little time to chat about non-work issues, but Amelia herself had a fair idea of the state of play in most of the staff's love lives, without being able to pinpoint how she *did* know.

So she'd shrugged off the irritated feeling, telling herself Mac probably knew she was available in the same way she knew Sally was about to become engaged. An osmosis kind of thing.

'I thought we'd better talk.'

Mac was standing outside as she emerged, though the room was used by both sexes and by doctors as often as by nurses, mainly because the doctors' locker room was a lot further down the corridor and so close to the kitchens it was usually uncomfortably hot.

'About the in-service training? I've a file of ideas, I'll get them to you. The main thing is—'

He interrupted her with a more ferocious than usual scowl.

'Not about your idea—about tomorrow night.'

'Oh!'

Amelia stared at him, unable to imagine what he could possibly need to tell her. It was apparently a work-related function, and if she didn't know by now how to behave at such things, she couldn't imagine learning much from Mac!

'So I thought I'd pick you up. At your place. Maybe a bit early so we could talk before we get there.'

If it hadn't been Mac standing in front of her, she'd have thought he was uncertain—but Mac was never uncertain.

'What about? Some special Mac-rules? Not to drink too much and embarrass you? Not to spill the dip over the medical superintendent? I *can* handle myself in social situations, Mac, though if you're having second thoughts, that's OK with me—providing you keep your word about the MAC meeting.'

'It's not that,' he said—definitely uneasy. 'It's other things. Say seven o'clock at your place. We'll go somewhere and have a drink first. Or we could have a drink at Capriccio's, only earlier. No, somewhere else. Is there anywhere you fancy?'

Amelia studied him for a minute as she puzzled over this most un-Mac-like behaviour. Clear olive-toned skin, straight nose, no-nonsense chin—he certainly looked like Mac.

'If you want to run through some ground rules you might as well have a drink at my place,' she suggested. 'In fact, if drinks are likely to be offered with dinner, it might be an idea to leave your car in the visitors' car park at my place and we can walk from there to Capriccio's.'

'We can?'

Uneasy was one thing—downright stupid was another. It was too much for Amelia.

'Mac, what's wrong with you?' she demanded. 'You know where I live. You've dropped me back at my apartment building when my car was out of action and we'd both been on late shift, or there was an extra late staff meeting. It's two blocks from Capriccio's. I assumed that's why, when you first mentioned it, you said you'd meet me there.'

Mac looked at the small female almost bursting with exasperation in front of his eyes, but if he'd sounded confused—which he obviously had—that wasn't the half of it. Confused didn't begin to cover the turmoil in his head, which had begun in the early hours of the morning and grown steadily worse ever since.

'That's great, then,' he said quickly, knowing if he hesitated he'd probably blurt out all he had to say right here and now, and she'd decide she wasn't going through with it and he'd be dateless. And Helene, being Helene, would see through any feeble excuse he might manage to conjure up. 'Seven—your apartment.'

Peterson gave him a look highly charged with suspicion but in the end nodded agreement and turned away, striding purposefully down the corridor. Mac watched her go, but it wasn't until the exit door swung closed behind her that he realised he didn't know her apartment number.

Perhaps there'd be names on the bells at the entrance.

He'd just decided that when the door swung open again.

'It's apartment number eight one three, eighth floor,' she called to him. 'Key in the numbers at the security gate and I'll buzz you in. You have to ring again from the front door as well, but my name's on the bell.'

With that settled he retreated to his office, meaning to make some inroads into the piles of paperwork. But in-

stead, he sat at his desk and thought about the 'talk' he'd
have to have with Peterson.

He should never have asked her.

He should have gone alone.

But Peterson was a good sport.

She'd understand.

Wouldn't she?

Mac still hadn't resolved that question to his satisfaction
when he finally rode up in the lift to the eighth floor of
the apartment building the next evening. Though he'd
been vaguely aware that the place where he'd occasionally
dropped Peterson off was an upmarket development, it
wasn't until he entered the ornate, marble, gold and palm-
adorned foyer that he'd realised how upmarket.

Had Peterson—whom he somehow knew had once
been married—done as well from her marriage settlement
as Helene had?

The thought irritated him but it did serve to divert his
mind from the talk—though only momentarily.

As the lift doors opened on eight, the door opposite
opened.

Mac smiled politely at the gorgeous young woman who
stood there and looked vaguely around the foyer, wondering which of the other three apartments was Peterson's.

'If you don't get out the doors will close and you'll be
swept back down to the ground floor,' the stunning
woman, whom he'd just vaguely begun to connect with
Peterson, said.

In Peterson's voice.

He stepped out of the lift.

'Peterson?'

He couldn't help it, though he inwardly cringed as he
heard his disbelief echo around the small space.

'Were you expecting me to wear my uniform?' she said crisply, standing aside, presumably so he could walk into her apartment.

If he could get his legs moving, that was!

He managed, but only just, and not before he'd caught a glimpse of an alluring shadow of cleavage above the neckline of the black dress that clung to her slimness like body paint.

'Are they your own?'

Duh! Once again, the least appropriate comment possible had emanated from his lips!

Peterson, however, managed with aplomb, shutting the door and turning to face him.

'Of course not, Mac. Knowing I was going out with you, I had breast implants inserted last night.'

Then she laughed.

'I *am* a woman, and most of us have breasts,' she said in a more kindly tone. 'And the engineering wonders of a good bra will produce cleavage in even the most mammarily challenged amongst us. What would you like to drink? I've beer, wine—red or white—whisky. Mac?'

The last questioning word was obviously because he was staring at her. He was past the point where he could see the shadowed cleavage and now realised why he'd not recognised her. It was the hair.

'It's your hair,' he said, letting his thoughts stray into words once again. Though it wasn't the hair—rather than bunched, it was held loosely at the nape of her neck in a gold clasp, with the unexpected length of it tumbling down her back in soft, shining curls—but the way not having her usual hairstyle made the bones of her face more defined.

Made her beautiful.

'Everyone has it.' The succinct reply didn't help, but

when she repeated her earlier request about drinks, he managed to pull himself together sufficiently to agree to whisky.

'Water? Ice? Soda?'

Easy questions, but she crossed the spacious living room as she asked, and her body moved sinuously beneath the painted-on dress.

'Mac?'

Amelia hid the laughter that longed to escape. When Mac had asked her out, she'd decided she'd go all out in the 'dressing-up' department, determined to let him see that she wasn't just an efficient uniform.

If his witless behaviour since arriving was any indication, she'd succeeded beyond her wildest dreams. But he'd better come down to earth soon, or the evening would be a nightmare—he gaping, and she repeating everything several times.

'Mac, it's just me, Peterson.' She crossed the room and patted his arm. 'You must have assumed I'd scrub up all right or you wouldn't have asked me out.' Another pat. 'Now, what would you like in your whisky? Water, soda, ice?'

The hazel eyes blinked, and though the stunned expression on his face lessened slightly, it didn't disappear altogether.

'Soda and ice,' he said, not looking at her face now but down to where, she knew, the deep, satin-trimmed V of her neckline revealed the soft, uplifted mounds of her breasts.

'Soda and ice it is,' she said cheerfully, allowing herself a slight chuckle as she crossed the room to the small drinks cabinet and fridge skilfully concealed in a wall of bookshelves. It was good to get one up on Mac.

She poured his drink and a glass of wine for herself,

then walked back towards where he stood, watching her with the wariness of a cat in new territory, unsure about possible dangers lurking in the vicinity.

'Most people comment on the view,' she said, handing him his whisky and waving her hand towards the wall of glass, beyond which the night lights blinked, strobed and shimmered, turning the city into a mystical, magical place.

She led the way to where deep leather armchairs were positioned to appreciate the outlook.

Fortunately, he followed. If he hadn't, she wasn't sure what she'd have done next. It was one thing to surprise Mac, but to turn him to a gaping statue…

Mac took a large gulp of the whisky, realising, too late, that it was, firstly, very good quality, and, secondly, more whisky than soda. But the shock of the liquid burning in his throat recalled him to where he was—and why he was there.

'It's a fantastic view,' he said, managing, for the first time since his arrival, to sound like his usual self. Physically, he wasn't quite there yet, but once he got used to Peterson looking so—well, different he'd be OK. 'Nice place. Part of your marriage settlement?'

He knew even before he heard Peterson's gasp of disbelief that he'd said the wrong thing—again!

'I'm sorry, I don't know why I said that,' he mumbled, throwing caution to the wind and taking another gulp of the drink. 'It's all connected to tonight, but it was still unpardonably rude and it's none of my business—'

'Oh, for heaven's sake, stop apologising, Mac!' Peterson said crossly. 'I'm not angry, though I should be. But so there's no misunderstanding, no, it isn't part of a marriage settlement but my own apartment, paid for with my own mortgage and being paid off by me and no one else. The only advantage I had was that our family company built the complex so I'm paying it off to the company rather than to a bank.'

He was about to apologise again when he realised that might make her really angry, so he sipped his drink instead—it was *very* good whisky—and wondered how to raise the subject he wished to discuss.

'It's not getting any earlier, Mac.' Peterson took the initiative. 'If you've something to say, now's the time.'

Mac looked at her—at the slim, svelte beauty with dark eyes dominating the wide-cheekboned, pointy-chinned face. When he'd practised this speech, it had been the real Peterson sitting across from him and, though it hadn't been easy, he'd managed it OK.

But now?

'Mac?'

Even her voice was different. He heard the echo of his name in his head and wondered if she'd always had that slightly husky tone that suggested—

'The thing is, Peterson,' he said, launching into speech in an attempt to rein in libidinous thoughts. 'What we're actually doing tonight is having dinner with my ex-wife. She's bringing someone she wants me to meet and she kind of assumed I'd be dating someone so she told me to bring her, but, you see, if she's about to marry this someone special she wants me to meet, and I didn't have a date, well, I'd look pathetic, wouldn't I? I mean, she'd be moving on with her life and I'd be still alone... That's when I thought of you.'

'Pathetic—me! Yes, I guess I can make the connection, but it's hardly flattering, Mac.'

The teasing smile accompanying the words told him she was joking, but it did something else totally unexpected. It stirred bits of him that hadn't stirred—well, not much—

for some time, and the thought of his body reacting to Peterson, of all people, sent his mind into another spin.

'I didn't mean you're pathetic,' he blustered. 'I meant me. *I* would have seemed pathetic, and it would have given her a chance to be all consoling—poor Mac, no one to love him—or, worse, to think I might actually not be dating because no one measures up to her. Yes, that's more likely the way Helene's mind would work. Did I tell you her name was Helene? Helene Clinton. She always kept her maiden name. Anyway, she never believed I was as relieved to be out of the marriage as she was. Marriage! The whole thing's a farce—an institution set up by people on the lookout for a new way to make money.

'Think about it, Peterson. Think of all the people who make a living out of the frills and falderals of marriage. Even ministers, who you'd think, if they wanted people wed in the eyes of God, would at least do it for nothing— as part of their ministerial duty. But they don't come cheap. And ribbons for the pews! Can you imagine anything more useless than—'

'Mac?'

The slightly bemused look on Peterson's face alerted him to the fact that, once again, he'd got carried away.

'If you want to tell me something specific,' she continued, speaking slowly and carefully so he'd be sure to understand, 'then say it now. You can give me your views on marriage and ribbons on church pews some other time.'

Her tone suggested 'some other time' was only the remotest of possibilities.

He stared at her, at this new Peterson, and shook his head, knowing there was no easy way.

'The thing is, Peterson…'

'You already said that!' She smiled again, which didn't help his concentration one bit.

'I know I did,' he said, 'but that's how I practised starting so I need it to get launched. The thing is, Peterson, I wondered if you'd mind if we kind of made out we were…um…er…dating, I suppose. You know, as if we liked each other—were kind of a couple.'

'What kind of a couple, Mac?'

He glared at her, knowing full well she understood exactly what he was asking.

'Any kind!' he snapped. 'Just a together-for-a-while kind of a couple—not on a first date.'

Another smile, this one tweaking up lips glossed in such a way they looked wet and very lickable.

Lickable? Kissable?

'But it's not a date,' she said gently, bringing him back to earth with a thud. Then she laughed, stood up and crossed to stand in front of him.

'OK, I know what you mean,' she relented. 'Do you want me to be madly in love or just a little? Hopelessly besotted, or simply deeply attracted? Should I moon? Fix my eyes on your every movement? Agree with everything you say?'

She shook her head. 'No, I couldn't go that far, but I can do a good ''devoted dog'' kind of look. See.'

She gazed down at him, her dark brown eyes velvety with an emotion he knew damn well she wasn't feeling, but as a 'devoted dog' look, he had to admit it was excellent.

'I don't think we need go that far,' he said, telling himself the eyes couldn't possibly have looked velvety. 'Helene knows I'd throw up if someone kept looking at me like that.'

Peterson grinned at him.

'That's good, because I don't think I could have kept it up. I'd keep remembering the times you've made me furious in A and E and end up with the dog-about-to-bite look instead. But the occasional agreement, a pat here or there, a slight brush of fingers—that's really all we need to get the meaning across.'

Mac nodded his agreement, although the idea of Peterson's slim, pink-nailed fingers brushing across any portion of his skin was activating his body once again.

He looked up at her, astonished for the zillionth time this evening. This time because it had been so easy, not the telling her, but her agreement—her understanding.

'Thanks, Peterson,' he said, and he meant it, though she obviously didn't realise just how heartfelt the word was from the way she was laughing.

'That's OK, McDougal,' she responded when she'd recovered enough to speak. She took a sip of her drink, her eyes holding his over the rim of the glass. 'But perhaps you should practise calling me by my first name—no amount of touching and mooning looks will work if you keep saying ''Peterson'' at me in your usual brusque manner.'

'Brusque?' She was right about the Peterson thing, but before he could agree he felt compelled to argue over the adjective. 'Me, brusque?'

She laughed again, moving away from him and slumping into an armchair, the better to enjoy her own mirth.

'Would you prefer rude?' she teased, eyes sparkling with a delight he'd seen before but had never realised was quite so attractive. 'Admit it, Mac, you're hardly the world's most diplomatic man.'

'I'm usually busy,' he said, although he knew it was no excuse. 'And I find it easier to keep people at arm's length—not get too involved. You know how it is, Peterson, because you're just the same.'

She looked at him and shook her head, but more in disbelief than in denial, then those glossy lips parted in another teasing smile and she said, 'My name's Amelia. Do you want to practise it?'

CHAPTER THREE

AMELIA walked beside Mac down the familiar street, the short journey made something akin to a voyage of adventure by the situation in which she found herself.

Inside, the giggles that had been present since he'd stumbled and mumbled his request that she put on a lover-like act still threatened to erupt, but though she smiled, she felt enough empathy with his plight to keep them to herself.

He'd taken her arm as they'd left the building but, apart from occasionally muttering 'Amelia' under his breath—probably willing himself to remember it—he hadn't spoken and she was sufficiently bemused by the situation to let the silence lie between them.

But as they walked into Lakelands' classiest restaurant, and a noisy group at the bar started calling out—'Hey, it's the Bug! What's happening, Bug? Who's the fella?'—Mac's hand tightened protectively and he moved so his body was between her and the dinner-suited young men.

'It's all right,' she told him. 'They're harmless. Just my youngest brother and some of his friends. I'll have to say hello.'

She moved towards the group, aware Mac was following, mainly because she could hear him repeating 'Bug?' under his breath. The giggle rose again. Poor man, he was having any number of shocks tonight.

She reached the bar, accepted kisses and over-the-top compliments from Rowley's mates, then introduced them all to Mac.

'And what are you lot celebrating—all dressed up to the nines?' she asked.

Rowley gave her a look of mock reproof.

'Don't tell me you've forgotten?' he said. 'It's the anniversary of Elvis's death. We're having a wake.'

'They're all mad,' Amelia explained to Mac. 'They've been Elvis fans since they were about seven and my misguided mother, also a fan, threw an Elvis party for Rowley's birthday. Back then, it was dressing up in glitter suits that got them in, but now they swear it's the music, though I think it's an excuse to throw a party. They celebrate his birthday, his first public performance, his first single, everything they can think of.'

All five young men now joined in, protesting it had always been the music, and Mac found himself smiling at their youthful exuberance, while wondering if he'd ever been *that* young—or so exuberant over anything!

'Well, we'll leave you to it,' Peterson—no, he had to call her Amelia—said, extracting them both before the conversation became too involved. The farewells reminded him of the greetings and as the *maître d'* showed them to their table, he caught Amelia's arm, holding her back long enough to ask.

'Bug?'

She grinned at him.

'Amelia—'Melia—mealie bug. I'm not sure which of my brothers started it, but all of them—and all their friends—have always called me Bug.'

'And you don't object?'

Mac looked incredulously down at the beautiful woman, but she was obviously unperturbed.

In fact, she smiled again as she answered.

'With four brothers, you learn to choose the battles you

fight. Being called Bug never bothered me enough to make an issue of it. They mean it kindly, you know.'

Mac shook his head, then, realising the *maître d'* was now well ahead of them, he took Amelia's arm and followed.

He could see Helene—tall, blonde, immaculately groomed and as beautiful as ever—sitting at a small, round table in the corner. And with her, an elegant-looking man, with smoothly slicked-back reddish-blond hair.

'So,' he said, moving closer to Amelia and resting his hand on her shoulder.

He felt her start at the touch, then she turned and looked enquiringly back at him.

'I guessed it'd be a man she wanted me to meet, and I was right.'

Amelia saw the fierceness in Mac's eyes and heard the edge of anger in his voice, and realised he probably still loved the woman they were about to deceive. Her heart tightened at the thought of him being unhappy and she lifted her hand and covered his where it still rested on her shoulder.

The *maître d'* was waiting for them again, and as Mac's touch urged her forward, she glanced back up at him again, and smiled with all her heart.

'Let the game begin,' she whispered, and was pleased to see the fierceness fade and Mac's more usual expression of cynical amusement take its place.

Introductions, brisk on Mac's part—'Helene, this is Amelia, Amelia, Helene,'—and cloyingly sweet on Helene's—'Mac, I'd like you to meet Troy Helman. Troy's a lobbyist for the Business Federation,'—didn't take long, and though Helene acknowledged Amelia's presence, she seemed far more eager to impress Mac with the wonderful man she'd won than interested in the woman he was seeing.

'I've always wondered what lobbyists do,' Amelia said, as she settled into the seat beside Troy. 'Of course, I know they represent special interest groups, and are used to influence government decisions, but if these decisions are important enough, shouldn't the government be making them anyway?'

The blond man smiled condescendingly at her.

'It's really far more complicated than that,' he said, and Amelia, who, possibly because of her lack of height, had been condescended to by experts, smiled.

'I'm sure it is,' she said sweetly, 'otherwise you wouldn't be paid such huge sums of money.'

She glanced superstitiously behind her to make sure her mother wasn't lurking nearby. She'd have been shocked to hear someone's income being mentioned over the dinner table.

'And what do you do, Emily?' Helene asked, leaning forward towards Amelia and taking the opportunity to rest her hand on one of Troy's.

'Amelia.'

Mac and Amelia chorused her correct name, then Amelia found herself wanting to giggle again, the situation was so farcical.

'She's a professor of electrical engineering at Lakelands U,' Mac said, lifting Amelia's hand to his lips and giving it, instead of a kiss, a nip of warning to play along. 'You wouldn't think it to look at her, would you?'

He gazed proudly at his companion, who, aware a darting look of horror might be intercepted, simply smiled modestly.

The drinks waiter interrupted the conversation, and by the time they'd all ordered—Mac had insisted on a glass of champagne for Amelia, and requested a whisky for himself while the other two were sticking soberly to mineral water—the menus had arrived and deciding what to eat took precedence over conversation.

Amelia was tossing up between a seafood risotto and a pasta dish for her main course when Mac leaned towards her and slid his arm around her shoulders.

It wasn't the first time he'd touched her this evening, but for some reason the feel of his fingers on her bare flesh started goose-bumps rising on her skin.

'Have you decided?' he asked, bending intimately towards her. 'And does it matter as far as wine's concerned? Would you like red or white? Something special?'

She turned and looked into his eyes, so close, and something inside her shifted, as if an anchor had been released.

This is Mac, she reminded herself. And it's all pretend.

'Dry white,' she said, then because her voice sounded husky with the strange tension she was feeling, and Helene might notice it, she looked lovingly into his eyes and added, 'You know the one I like, darling.'

'Darling' seemed taken aback, but only momentarily.

'Great!' he said, smiling at her as if she'd just been extraordinarily clever, then he turned to the hovering drinks waiter, who'd just delivered the first order, and ordered a bottle of French pinot, which Amelia knew from other visits to Capriccio's was the most expensive still white wine on the menu.

'We might have preferred a red,' Helene said, with enough ice in her voice to make Amelia shiver.

'Oh, that's OK,' Mac said, waving his hand carelessly in the air. 'I'm just ordering for the two of us—you go right ahead and get whatever you like.'

He lifted his whisky and took a deep draught, making

Amelia wonder if maybe the pre-dinner drink he'd had at her place had already gone to his head and she was about to see the uptight Fraser McDougal a little on the tipsy side.

The thought made her want to giggle again, but in Helene's ultra-sophisticated company she thought better of it.

A little on the tipsy side? Amelia thought later. She was certainly that way herself. A glass of champagne and two glasses of white wine, plus a glass of dessert wine with the slice of seven-layer Viennese torte she'd had after her risotto, was way, way beyond her usual limits.

Perhaps more than a little tipsy, she decided as she laughed at some ridiculous tale Mac was telling. Though perhaps part of the unreality she felt was to do with Mac, rather than the wine, for the man sitting beside her, touching her lightly on the arm, the hand, the shoulder, whispering silly comments in her ear, was as different to the Mac she knew at work as…

Well, as different as she was to Helene.

Helene had dominated most of the conversation, sprinkling every sentence with the names of politicians and high-powered business people, but whether from habit or because she wanted to impress Mac, Amelia couldn't decide.

It certainly hadn't been to impress Amelia, who had been studiously ignored by Helene throughout the meal. Troy had been kinder, turning to her to try to draw her in, but as political discussions and the intricacies of political wrangling bored her rigid, Amelia had been happy to be left out.

Troy had even tried a few halting questions about electrical engineering, but as he probably knew a lot more than Amelia did on the subject—she wasn't sure if being able to change a fuse counted—she'd sidestepped his conversational gambits with a comment about the deliciousness of her meal and a harmless question about whether Canberra, where he was now based, had always been his home.

They were preparing to leave when Rowley drifted across to their table, and a sister's knowing eye guessed he'd been celebrating the anniversary of The King's death a bit too hard.

'Catch up with you soon, Bug,' he said, bending to drop a kiss on his sister's cheek and, under cover of the gesture, adding, 'Very soon! You know I'll have to report to the others about this Mac guy.'

He strolled away, while Amelia sighed—realising she'd be fielding questions about Mac for the next few weeks.

'Wasn't that Rowley Peterson?'

Helene's eyes narrowed suspiciously as she asked Amelia the question.

'Yes, do you know him?' Amelia said, all innocence.

'He's Amelia's brother,' Mac explained, but *his* innocence was real. It had been obvious, when Amelia had introduced them earlier, that Mac had never heard of Australia's newest young singing star.

'But I read where he's one of the United Construction Petersons,' Helene said, staring suspiciously at Amelia.

So? she wanted to say, but she'd already let her manners desert her a couple of times this evening.

Instead, she said nothing. Her family's company might be one of the top ten businesses in the state, but what they did or didn't do was none of Helene's business. Besides, Mac was now looking curiously at her, and if it became apparent that he didn't know her background, the evening's charade would be pointless.

She leaned towards him and rested her weight against his body, and looked up, through languorously lowered lids, into his eyes.

'I think it might be nearly time for bed, darling,' she murmured, pitching her voice just loud enough for the other two to hear.

She felt Mac's jolt of reaction, but he recovered well, dealing out a jolt of his own when he wrapped his arms around her, then bent his head and dropped a light kiss on her lips.

'Your wish is my command,' he murmured, the huskiness of his voice vibrating down her spine.

It's all pretend, Amelia reminded herself, but other parts of her were remembering how long it had been since she'd found pleasure in a man's arms.

'Professor of electrical engineering!' she said to Mac when they'd settled the account, said their goodbyes and were walking, arms slung companionably—and perhaps slightly tipsily—around each other's waists, down the street to her apartment. 'Where on earth did that come from?'

Mac gave a great shout of laughter.

'Brilliant, wasn't it? You should have seen your face. But Helene's not only a people snob—you'd have gathered that from the name-dropping—but an intellectual one as well. She thinks being brighter than the average person gives her all kinds of advantages. I had to cut her down to size or she'd have patronised you all evening.'

'So, instead, she ignored me,' Amelia said. 'Is she still in love with you that she feels so threatened?'

'Threatened? Helene? No way! And as for being in love with me, that's a laugh. She's the one who instigated divorce proceedings, you know. She felt I wasn't moving fast enough or far enough up the career ladder. As far as she was concerned, A and E was a dead end. But while we're on the subject of conversational topics, what does that brother of yours do that Helene knew of him, and who the hell are United Construction?'

He stopped and turned Amelia to face him.

'Who are you, Amelia Peterson?'

She laughed, and shook her head.

'You know exactly who I am, Mac. What you see is what you get with me. The family's construction business is big enough to be known beyond Lakelands, so most people have heard of it, and Rowley sings. He's a teenage pop idol but he's also into songs older people enjoy. The boys he was with—they're members of his band.'

She studied him for a moment, then added, 'He's...I suppose famous is the word, but it's hard to think of your kid brother as famous. But even people like Helene, who I imagine isn't a pop music fan, would know of him and recognise his face, so how come you've missed out? You don't read papers?'

He didn't answer for a long moment, and when he did she realised most of this, to her way of thinking, quite lucid explanation must have gone right over his head.

'But that's just it,' he said. 'What I saw wasn't what I got. Or maybe that should have been, what I thought I saw...'

Mac was still staring at her, his face perplexed, then the arm, which had remained around her waist, tightened and his hand drew her up against his body. There was a long, tense pause, then he bent and kissed her.

Part of Amelia registered that it had been a long time since she'd been kissed in the main street of Lakelands— a long time since she'd been kissed anywhere for that matter. Then the kiss took effect with a sizzle of sheer excitement that started somewhere down in the region of her toes and simmered up through her body to lodge in her chest where it triggered such havoc in her heart that that usually reliable organ banged against her ribs with a heavy thudding rhythm.

A spatter of applause broke the spell, and Amelia looked around to find the previously deserted street was now well populated—had a movie just ended? Had anyone she knew seen their behaviour? Not that Mac seemed perturbed—he straightened up but kept a firm grip around Amelia's waist as he steered her on their way.

Just as well he did, as her legs had lost their ability to hold her upright—which, given her companion, she decided to blame on the alcohol she'd consumed, rather than the kiss.

Somehow they made their way back to her apartment where, without conversation or consideration, the kiss resumed, firing an aching need in Amelia that overcame all restraint or common sense. In what seemed a totally natural, if somewhat hurried progression, they moved towards her bedroom, shedding clothes as their hands sought more contact with each other's bodies, and their excitement grew.

A long time later, Amelia woke, curled against Mac's strong warm body.

'Unexpected, huh?' he said, his deep voice raising goose-bumps on her skin.

He was propped on one elbow, one hand smoothing her hair against the pillow, his face, lit by a shaft of light from her bathroom, softer than she'd ever seen it.

'Very,' she agreed, trying to be as matter-of-fact about this bizarre situation as he was. Then honesty prompted her to add, 'But very nice.'

'Only very nice?' he teased, running his fingers lightly across her breast. 'Only very nice?'

The teasing fingers drifted lower and within minutes their excitement had built again, not to be denied.

But this time it was a slower, more languorous loving, and when desire was satisfied they didn't sleep, but lay, pressed against each other, talking desultorily, conversation ranging from work to family, then back to work again. It was inevitable their pasts would come into the conversation, Mac pointing out that though he'd explained how his marriage had broken up through the hours he worked and his determination to remain in A and E, he knew nothing about hers.

'It seems like ancient history,' Amelia said, relishing the physical repleteness that led to total relaxation. 'I married young, halfway through my nursing course. Brad was a friend of my brothers, he worked for my father in the construction business, and getting married was like a natural next step somehow, but nothing happened. Nothing got better, and though we didn't fight, we just kind of drifted apart.'

She turned, and splayed her hand flat across Mac's broad chest.

'We'd been married for five years and though, all through, we'd been trying to have a child, it didn't happen. I know now it would have been a disaster. We were better off apart. Brad's remarried now, and we see each other occasionally—no hard feelings, no hassles.'

'And since? Why no man in your life, Peterson?'

He was threading his fingers through her hair now, as if the length of it could be judged by feel.

Amelia shrugged, mostly in an attempt to shake off the vibrations those delving fingers had prompted.

'No one's come along who was worth making an effort

for,' she said, surprising herself with her honesty. 'Relationships do take an effort, don't they?'

The chest beneath her fingers rose and fell as Mac heaved a long sigh.

'They do indeed,' he said. Then he added, in funereal tones, 'And *time*!'

'Exactly,' Amelia agreed, but against all odds her body was coming back to life, and only a little exploration told her Mac's was also stirring.

'It's impossible,' he protested. 'I'm an aging man!'

'Ho! All of thirty-five! Poor old fellow!'

So this time, as they made love, they were light-hearted, teasing and joking and smiling through the passion.

And this time, sleep came again, a sleep so deep Amelia didn't hear Mac leave. But when she woke, close to midday, she was alone in her bed, the vague but not unpleasurable aches in her body the only reminder of the extraordinary night.

She sat up, wondering if he'd gone, then saw the note on the pillow next to hers.

Believe me, Peterson, I'd much rather have stayed, but I woke at nine forty-five and remembered, panic-stricken, that my father's away and I was supposed to collect my mother at ten to take her to church—new niece's christening, would you believe? Thank you for a very special night, Mac.

Amelia read it several times, trying hard to imagine Mac with a mother and father, and either a brother or a sister. Maybe he had both.

Were they like him?

She shook her head, smiling at her own absurdity. She

didn't really know what Mac was like—outside work—so how could she possibly imagine his family?

She read the note again, ignoring his reason for leaving.

The last sentence appeared to draw a line under their relationship—if you could call dinner and a night of totally unexpected pleasure and passion a relationship. The message behind that undoubtedly genuine 'thank you' was 'that's it'. Which was OK with her—after all, she'd only been doing Mac a favour, in return for one for herself. The fact that she'd enjoyed it—all of it—was just a bonus!

Monday at work proved her suppositions correct. Mac was already in the department when she arrived and the first thing she heard was his voice issuing rapid-fire orders to some poor unfortunate in a curtained-off cubicle.

The unfortunate turned out to be a student nurse doing work placement—or so Amelia surmised when the young woman emerged with tears streaming down her cheeks. Amelia stepped towards her, but before she could offer a touch or word of comfort she was paged, the code suggesting an urgent emergency admittance due to arrive within minutes.

She met the ambulance as it pulled in, listening as the female ambulance attendant gave her a brief but concise rundown on the case.

'Four-year-old burn victim, fire could have started in his bedroom. We intubated him six minutes ago. Parents are on their way to the Royal in another ambulance, but he'll need to go into the children's burns ICU here at St Pat's.'

Amelia checked the child as she helped a porter wheel him into the nearest trauma cubicle. As well as the endotracheal tube into his lungs, a nasogastric tube had been inserted into his left nostril. A sixteen-gauge intraosseus line had been inserted into his lower left leg—part of his body not obviously affected by burns—and fluid was flowing into his body through this. Burns to his face and neck suggested the child had been close to the seat of the fire so inhalation injury could be present.

'I'll take over the bag,' Amelia said to the second attendant, who was pressing oxygen into the child's lungs by squeezing a ventilation bag. Then she turned to a junior nurse who'd arrived to assist her. 'Get a respiratory technician here to do this and have another call put out for a doctor. Who the hell was supposed to answer that code?'

'I was.' A flustered young man Amelia had never seen before appeared through the gap in the curtain. 'Bring me up to date.'

Maybe not so flustered, she thought, registering the bossy note in his voice.

The attendant who'd been ventilating the child handed the doctor the sheet containing all the information collected thus far, then escaped from the cubicle.

'Estimated weight of eighteen kilograms and they've inserted a four-millimetre endotracheal tube?' he said. 'Eighteen kilograms should have been a five. Don't these people have a chart for weights and tube sizes?'

'The child's badly burnt around the face and neck so inhalation injury is almost certainly present,' Amelia said, remaining calm although the doctor's attitude irritated her. 'It causes oedema, swelling in the upper airway, peaking in six to eight hours. An ETT a size smaller is usually recommended if there's a risk of inhalation problems, but right now shouldn't you be checking his chest—making sure it's been correctly inserted and is clear of obstruction or kinking?'

'Don't tell me about oedema or what to do, Nurse,' the

young man snapped, but he did listen to the child's chest and draw blood for a blood-gas determination.

He checked the fluid flowing into the child's leg, then worked out, using the patient's assumed weight, what extra fluid should be given, and how often. Knowing the child needed massive fluid resuscitation, Amelia was pleased when he sought another site for a second large-bore catheter to be inserted.

The respiratory technician arrived at the same time as the blood-gas results, and saw them before the young doctor.

'This suggests inadequate ventilation,' the therapist said, handing the slip to the doctor. 'I'll suction out the tube and then connect the oxygen directly to the source.'

Amelia turned to the cupboard for a paediatric suction kit, washing her hands and putting on clean gloves before opening it and setting it up on a trolley beside the therapist. Although she could do this procedure, having someone present who had done probably hundreds of them, made the job safer and simpler.

The young doctor, in the meantime, had inserted a second fluid line into the child's right leg.

'Though how the hell we're going to secure it I don't know,' he muttered, and Amelia, seeing the burnt flesh around the catheter, realised that the usual gauze and tape would be useless.

'I'll tie it there,' she offered, and the doctor stepped back, ordering the nurse who'd returned with the blood-gas results to set up more bags of fluid. This was followed by a string of other orders, given too quickly, Amelia was sure, for the young nurse to follow.

Amelia was wrapping gauze bandage around the catheter, ready to secure it by tying it around the child's leg, when she realised the left leg, where the original line had been inserted, was swelling alarmingly.

'You've got a problem here,' she said quietly to the doctor, pointing to the swollen leg. 'The line's obviously blocked for some reason. It should come out before it causes complications. Can you find a new site?'

'Who do you think I am—Superman?' he snapped. 'I'm trying to insert a catheter to monitor the fluid resuscitation. Severe burns, the child's in shock, we've got to pump fluid into him and you're suggesting we remove one of the lines?'

Amelia could feel panic fluttering in her heart. The young doctor was probably extremely capable but he was out of his depth in this particular situation, and though she knew she could take over a lot of the tasks he was expected to do, he was resentful of her interference. By now, someone from the burns unit should have arrived. Someone with experience and expertise in burns.

'We need a new ABG. From the look of the child he's still getting insufficient ventilation,' the respiratory tech said, referring to the blood-gas test they'd run earlier. 'I've checked all the equipment and raised the volume of oxygen, but he doesn't look good.'

'Doesn't look good,' the doctor muttered. 'Great diagnosis!'

He turned to Amelia.

'Take more blood and get it tested.'

Amelia didn't argue, but as she handed the vial to the aide who'd arrived to act as a runner, she whispered, 'Get Mac.'

Then, with gentle hands, she began to cut charred clothing off the child, removing anything not stuck to his skin. The degree of burning around his chest suggested there was a chance of circumferential burning. The dry crust, eschar, forming from the burn could have become a tight band, preventing chest expansion, and if his lungs couldn't expand inside his chest, then no amount of ventilation would help.

'No one from the burns unit here?'

Mac's voice brought relief flooding through Amelia.

'I've just finished three months up there—I told the triage sister I could manage,' the young doctor said, and Amelia waited for Mac to explode.

But he said nothing, merely moving into the room, seeing the burns on the child's chest, seizing the blood result as the runner came in, then ordering a scalpel for an escharotomy.

'You!' He caught the runner as she was retreating back towards the opening in the curtain. 'Get someone from the burns unit down here. Kevin, get another fluid line into this kid *now*! Peterson, remove the catheter from the left leg, it's obviously compromised.'

Amelia felt the terrible tension in her shoulders ease, and she hurried to obey, not because she was afraid of Mac's barked orders but because she knew whatever he ordered her to do was in the best interests of the child.

She watched as he cut through the constricting scar tissue around the child's chest, then took over the insertion of the second fluid line, this one into the lower end of the child's left femur. Shelley Bush, a young specialist intensivist and one of four permanent doctors in the burns unit, arrived as Mac stepped back, leaving the doctor he'd called Kevin to attach the fluid line.

'He ready to go, Mac?' Shelley asked, and Mac turned to the respiratory tech.

'You're happy?'

She nodded. 'I'll go with him and bag him on the way,'

she said, shifting the oxygen tube from the wall supply to the small cylinder on the gurney.

Amelia went into action, securing the drip stands to the gurney, checking all the tubes and lines they'd inserted into the little body were secure. She was aware of Mac's presence—aware of his body in a way she hadn't been before—but the severity of the child's injuries had banished any awkwardness that might have accompanied this first meeting since their totally unexpected intimacy the previous Saturday evening.

'Go up with them to keep an eye on the tubes,' Mac said to her, and she was happy to obey, the child still the sole focus of her attention.

She returned to find another crisis in full flow, voices calling for help from three cubicles.

'What's happening?' she demanded of the first nurse she saw.

'Kid rescued from a swimming pool in one, heart attack in two and a fellow who tried to cut his arm off with a circular saw in three.'

Amelia swore under her breath, then asked, 'Which one's the new intern in?'

'Three,' the nurse said, then she hurried off to complete whatever task had been asked of her.

She walked into three—and a scene of chaos.

'IV in his left arm has packed up, and doctor's trying to find a new vein,' the nurse just inside the curtains whispered at her.

Amelia mentally wished him luck as the patient was grossly overweight and accessible veins were often hard to find.

'Has Theatre been alerted?' she asked no one in particular, and won a glare from the doctor.

'Of course they have, but they won't have a theatre free

for twenty minutes so, rather than give unnecessary advice, why don't you make yourself useful and loosen that tourniquet? Keep pressure on the wound at the same time to prevent too much blood loss, then retighten it.'

The patient was grey and sweaty, obviously in shock. Amelia touched his feet—very cold and mottled-looking—and wanted to ask about shock trousers, an inflatable suit that could be wrapped around the legs and lower body to counteract hypotension, but one look at the doctor's face told her she'd better keep her mouth shut.

Another look at the patient told her that was wrong.

'What about shock trousers? Wouldn't they help restore his blood pressure while he's waiting for the op?'

The young intern glared again.

'If the paramedics thought he needed them, they'd have put them on!' he muttered. 'He's lost so much blood he needs fluids fast. That's my concern. IV first, urinary catheter second, then we'll look at how he's going.'

Amelia nodded, but she sent a nurse for a set of trousers which opened flat and could be fitted around a patient and secured with Velcro straps and zippers then inflated in sections. Fortunately, before she could get into an argument with the doctor over using them, two porters from Theatre arrived to take the patient upstairs.

'That Kevin's bloody hopeless,' she said, hours later, to Brian Stubbs, a senior nurse on duty with another A and E team.

They'd met up by the coffee-machine, which was so ancient it dispensed a variety of liquids according to its whim. Today's concoction, Amelia guessed, sniffing suspiciously at the murk in her paper cup, was a mix of tea and chocolate. Not appetising in any way, but hot and wet.

'So? You're the senior, do something about it,' Brian

said, pressing buttons on the machine, then sighing as he, too, sniffed his brew. 'And do something about this machine while you're at it. If you're going to take it to Mac, you might as well get a couple of complaints in before he bellows at you.'

'You take it to Mac,' Amelia said, as a shiver of something very like apprehension trickled down her spine.

'Take what to Mac? Coffee?'

'You mean tocalate,' Amelia said, turning around and pressing her cup into Mac's hands. 'Tea and chocolate mix. We need a new coffee-machine and a new intern. In either order, I don't care.' She looked up at him and the shiver intensified, so she fought it with more words. 'Well, yes, I do. At least the coffee-machine can only kill the staff—the intern could kill a patient. Change him first.'

She forced herself to keep her eyes on Mac's face, so saw a mobile eyebrow rise.

'In an exaggerative mood today, are we, Peterson?' he said smoothly. 'You know damn well the kid'll learn. First day today, and he was flustered. And you didn't help, bossing him around. He's already complained to me about your attitude.'

'*He's* complained about *me*?'

Amelia was aware her voice had risen an octave, but the statement was so outrageous she was surprised she could speak at all.

Mac's face, or what she could see of it now he'd lifted the cup and was sipping her revolting drink, remained bland.

'Says you were out of order, the way you spoke to him.'

Amelia rolled her eyes. 'I'll give the brat ''out of order'',' she muttered angrily.

'You'll treat him with respect,' Mac snapped. 'And that's an *order*, Peterson!'

She stared at him in disbelief. Mac was usually the first to complain about inexperienced staff in the A and E. She looked around for support, but Brian had eased away—or disappeared into thin air.

Left on her own to handle the ogre, she remembered the tearful nurse she'd seen when she'd arrived at work.

It had definitely been Mac's voice in that cubicle!

'Oh, yes?' she snapped right back at him. 'Well, in that case, what's sauce for the goose is sauce for the gander. You try treating my nurses with respect as well. The kid you had in tears this morning is still a student. From the look on her face when she came out of that cubicle, she might give up her studies right now.'

Mac frowned down at her, then shook his head.

'I haven't upset anyone this morning,' he said, and Amelia found her anger had vanished and, contrarily, she wanted to smile at the innocent confusion she could hear in Mac's voice.

But she wasn't going to let him off so easily. If you didn't stand up to Mac he steamrollered right over you. And if he thought one night of terrific sex was going to have her kowtowing to him, he could think again.

'First thing this morning,' Amelia said firmly. 'Young Allison Wright. The student. She came out of cubicle two in tears.'

'Ah!' Mac said, and a broad grin lit his craggy features.

The grin made an array of tendons tighten in Amelia's belly, as if it had tugged some strings inside her, but she ignored all that as best she could and continued to scowl at him so he'd know he hadn't answered.

'Tears, eh? Fancy that!' he added, then, with another smile, he turned and walked away.

CHAPTER FOUR

MAC sought refuge among his paper alps. He'd been dreading seeing Peterson this morning. In his experience, on the rare occasions when chance, and possibly overindulgence in alcohol, had led to an unexpected but still pleasurable sexual encounter, the woman in question had found it more difficult to handle afterwards than he had. Although he'd have said he knew Peterson quite well, Saturday night had put paid to that assumption and he had to admit he'd had no idea how she'd react.

So coming to work this morning, with thoughts of facing up to Peterson again, had been stressful to say the least.

Personally, of course, he could draw a line under the incident and file it tidily away.

'Just like all this paperwork,' he muttered sarcastically to himself. 'And who are you trying to fool? *Ordinarily* you can draw a line under it. But Peterson? Might take a while to forget that *incident*.'

'Talking to yourself again, Mac?'

The cause of his confusion breezed into the room, and while his pulse rate accelerated with concern over what she might have come to say, his body also reacted, mainly because he seemed to be seeing right through her rather crumpled uniform to the slim, porcelain-skinned and utterly desirable body he now knew lay beneath it.

'Well, I won't interrupt you—it's probably an important discussion. But I wanted to remind you that Enid Biggs is due back next week, so this week's MAC meeting is the last chance you'll have to raise the issue of in-service training for the A and E nurses.'

She positively smirked as she added, 'A bargain's a bargain, remember.' Then she turned and headed for the door.

But before exiting, she must have thought of something else, for she swung around.

'Oh, and I owe you an apology,' she said. 'I spoke to Allison, the student nurse, and she said she was crying because she'd just seen her first baby delivered, not because you yelled at her.'

And on that note, she departed.

Mac rubbed his eyes and stared at the space where Peterson had been. He knew she couldn't possibly have been naked as she'd walked out the door, but he was sure he'd seen a slim naked back and two pert buttocks swaying seductively into the hall.

It had to be shock.

Peterson apologising was enough to send anyone into shock.

But before that had been the shock of her coming in—something he'd been dreading. Kind of dreading…

But she hadn't even mentioned Saturday.

It wasn't natural. Women always wanted at least a small post-mortem, while most of them seemed to consider enjoyable indulgence in sex would lead inevitably into a relationship. It was one of the reasons he avoided casual sex.

More like avoided any sex, his libido reminded him.

He swiped a pile of papers onto the floor in sheer frustration. With himself for wasting time even thinking about the issue, and with Peterson for behaving as she was—acting as nothing had happened between them.

What was she made of?

Ice?

'Mac, have you got a form called an A4726?'

Colleen, his secretary, appeared in his doorway.

Fully clothed, so he wasn't seeing all females naked...

'Heavens, what *have* you done?'

She swooped on the spill of papers across the floor and started gathering them into a large bundle.

'Honestly, Mac, we've got to sort these out. How about I stay late tomorrow and we go through the lot together? You can tell me whether to file or shred and we'll get down to the surface of your desk.'

'In one evening? It'd take a month.'

Colleen sighed, though she knew it aggravated him to have her make that long-suffering noise.

'One evening might be a start. And why are you such a bear today? I thought after Petra's christening yesterday, you'd be all sweetness and light.'

She stopped stacking papers long enough to glance up at him. 'Well, maybe not that good, but at least bearable.'

Mac nodded to concede her point. Colleen had been with him for years, first as a general secretary in A and E and then moving into the position of his personal secretary when he was appointed director of the department. As a result, she knew him well—though how she'd discovered his utter fascination with his new niece, Mac had no idea.

He just hoped she'd keep it to herself. It certainly wasn't something he wanted publicised—the fact that he'd gone soppy over a newborn baby. The entire A and E department would take it as a sign of either senility or that he was cracking up.

'About the A4726?' Colleen said as she straightened up and dumped the pile of papers on his spare chair.

Mac sighed even more deeply than she had earlier.

'Let's hope we find it tomorrow night. The darned thing's already caused a heap of trouble.'

Colleen looked expectantly at him, but as he had no intention of explaining he ignored the silent query, instead agreeing that, yes, tomorrow evening would be a good time to make a start on sorting the paperwork.

But if Colleen had expected his mood to have improved, she was in for a shock. He'd spent the entire day trying to avoid Peterson, even going so far as to start sorting papers himself so he didn't keep bumping into her between cubicles. Yet she'd kept bobbing up—like one of those weighted blow-up toys that you could punch and hit and whack and it still bounced back.

Not that he wanted to punch, hit or whack Peterson, but there were numerous other things he'd never before considered doing with her which now seemed to have shifted to the forefront of his mind. While his eyes continued to see right through her clothes, and his fingers twitched with a need to loosen her hair from the knot arrangement she wore it in at work.

Damn the woman!

'There, we've reduced it down to a couple of piles, which you can clear away tomorrow,' Colleen announced.

It was after ten and, though they'd taken half an hour off their sorting to grab a sandwich and coffee earlier, Mac was starving.

'You want to go across the road to Mercurio's for some pasta?' he asked Colleen. 'My shout because you've been so helpful. And though you can claim overtime, we both know you've Buckley's chance of getting it.'

Colleen shook her head.

'No, I'm heading home for bed, and I'm going to take

a long lunch later in the week in lieu of overtime.' She eyed him sternly. 'That *is* all right, isn't it?'

'Of course it is,' he grumbled, put out by her refusal because, although he usually ate alone and didn't mind it, tonight he'd have welcomed company—any company— to stop his thoughts straying where they shouldn't stray. 'As if you need to ask.'

He set the A4726, which he'd found marking the place in a medical book he'd been reading, squarely on the desk, right in front of his chair, so he could deal with it first thing in the morning, then grabbed his jacket and walked out, nodding to staff who bustled past him but resolutely ignoring the usual behind-the-scenes chaos of the department.

At this time of night, Mercurio's was quiet, though Mac recognised a couple of tables of hospital staff—one of senior hospital staff.

Recognisably senior staff…

Damn and blast!

'Just coming off duty, Mac?' Phil Allen, head of the medical advisory committee, called to him. 'Want to join us and hear all the boring stuff we discussed at the meeting?'

Panic was churning in Mac's stomach by now. Could he join them and mention Peterson's idea? That way, he could tell her he'd brought it up.

Lie to Peterson?

'No!' he said, answering his thoughts but obviously startling Phil, so he added a quick, 'Thanks, anyway, but I'm only here for a take-away. Sorry I missed the meeting, but it's been hectic down there today.'

'Don't I know it,' Kel Roberts, a senior surgeon, said. 'Most of your intake seemed to end up in Theatre, though yesterday was worse. I think we saved that fat chap's arm, by the way.'

Mac chatted for a few minutes, then excused himself and moved away, part of his mind working sufficiently well to order a pizza with the works, while a far larger part flapped about in panic-stricken upheaval, wondering how it could possibly explain to Peterson he'd forgotten the MAC meeting.

Not that he needed to explain, as it turned out. She was waiting—with the A4726—in his office next morning, and the fire in her quite lovely brown eyes suggested she'd already heard.

'So, have you any excuse?' she demanded, putting paid to any hope he might be imagining things.

'I just forgot,' he said, trying hard to sound contrite, while fighting an extraordinary urge to kiss the tightly compressed lips back to their usual fullness. 'Colleen offered to stay back and help me sort the paperwork.'

He waved his hand towards the one remaining pile, neatly encapsulated in his in-tray.

'I'm sorry, Peterson, I really am, and I'll certainly bring it up in a fortnight and even fight the DON for you. I promise.'

Her clothes had disappeared again and his body throbbed with memory.

'You'd better!' she growled, and walked away, leaving him once again with a strange, spun-out-of-orbit sensation.

'She's not going to mention last Saturday night!' Speaking the thought aloud didn't make it less unbelievable. 'It's as if it never happened, as far as she's concerned.'

Which is how you wanted it to be, surely, he told himself, though he was beginning to doubt if he knew what he wanted.

Apart from another night with Peterson, of course...

Amelia walked away from Mac's office. When she'd bumped into Phil Allen in the canteen earlier and learnt Mac had missed the meeting, she'd been so mad she'd gone charging through the building, ready to rip his head off.

Well, maybe not rip his head off, but certainly do a bit of yelling. For a start, a good yell might release some of the tension working anywhere near him now caused. She'd told herself a thousand times that nothing had changed between them, but her body failed to grasp this fact and her nerve endings did excited little dances every time she heard his voice, while his physical presence resulted in complicated tangos in her abdomen and a flutter of waltzes in her lungs.

But when she'd walked into his office and seen the tidy desk, she'd realised just what an effort sorting all that paper must have been and her anger had ebbed away, replaced by the foolish wish that she might have been the one to help him.

As if! she'd upbraided herself, then, hearing his footsteps in the hall, she'd straightened her spine, donned the fiercest scowl she could muster and gone on the attack. There was no way he was going to guess what was going on inside her.

The stand-off continued for another nine days. A and E was as busy as usual, with the usual array of cases coming in through the doors. On the Friday, Amelia, who'd been congratulating herself on keeping out of Mac's way ninety per cent of the time, was called to a patient admitted by ambulance, unconscious but without obvious complaint or injury. Until they removed his clothes and found massive bruising on the skin across his belly, the result of some inexplicable accident or a severe beating.

'His blood pressure's dropping. I want a Guiac and UA,' Angus Rhyles, the resident on duty, said to Amelia as he listened for sounds in the patient's bowels.

Amelia gloved up and performed the simple task of obtaining a stool sample then testing it with developing solution. It turned a bright blue, proving there was blood in the bowels, which could be the result of a blunt trauma injury or disease.

She passed on the information to Angus, who was ordering a peritoneal lavage—fluid washed through the abdominal cavity then retrieved and checked for blood—and catheterised the patient to obtain a urine sample. This was sent off to the lab.

'Blood in his abdominal cavity—could be his spleen or liver, and the blood in the sample means his bowel could be torn as well,' Angus was saying, as Amelia, alerted to a further drop in blood pressure by the nurse who was watching the monitors, prepared a resuscitation tray.

She didn't need to be told whom Angus was addressing—the tightening of the nerves in her skin had already told her that.

'Let's sort out the BP first,' Mac said briskly. 'Peterson, get on to Theatre and tell them he'll be up in a few minutes—internal bleeding, possibly bowel damage and query peritonitis. And don't listen to any half-assed excuses about lack of staff or theatres—they've got the biggest budget in the hospital and have surgeons lying about in the on-call rooms half the day.'

Amelia left the cubicle, glad to escape. It had been

obvious from the start that as far as Mac was concerned their night of love-making might never have happened.

Well, that suited her just fine—and today it also made her just angry enough to yell at the theatre secretary who dared to suggest they keep the patient in A and E a little longer.

'He's on his way up now,' Amelia told her, and slammed the phone back in its cradle.

By the time she returned to the cubicle, two policemen had arrived, and while Mac worked to stabilise the man, Angus answered questions from the police about the patient's condition. He was careful only to explain what they'd found, and not draw conclusions as to the cause.

'OK, take him up,' Mac said, turning to a porter who was pressed back against the curtain. 'Peterson, you go with them in case anyone argues.'

One of the policemen objected and Mac turned on him.

'The bloke's unconscious—you can't question him!' he growled.

'But we have to stay with him,' the policeman replied.

'Then sit outside Theatre—just don't bother my staff.'

So both policemen accompanied the gurney up to the fourth floor, where Amelia left them arguing with the theatre secretary and retreated back to A and E.

A young man who'd had a fall on a building site had been admitted, deeply unconscious and with massive internal and external injuries. For the next three hours she worked under Mac's barked orders, but in the end the specialist trauma team of which she was part had to admit he was beyond their help.

By then the new shift had arrived, and the exhausted and emotionally depleted day-shift members who'd lost their patient made their way to the tearoom, where they all collapsed into chairs and stared blankly into space.

Mac was the first to speak.

'It happens, gang, you all know that. We did what we could, and it wasn't good enough, but that's not our fault.'

'It's harder at the end of the day,' Angus said, 'because you have the time to think about it. All the way home—all night. When it happens earlier in the day, you're too darned busy to worry about it.'

'Which isn't always good,' Amelia told him. 'Too much gets shut away, and that's how burn-out happens.'

'I just hate seeing young healthy people die in stupid accidents,' the respiratory tech, a young man Amelia hadn't met before, said. 'Makes you think too much about your own mortality.'

'Working in A and E has a tendency to do that,' Mac told him. 'So, what's the saying? Live for today?'

He rose stiffly to his feet.

'Peterson, can I see you in my office?'

The rest of them watched him leave the room, then turned to Amelia.

'You in trouble again, Peterson?' one of the nurses asked, while Angus cocked an eyebrow in her direction.

'Been bugging him about his attitude to your nurses?' he said.

Amelia, who had a host of her own questions to deal with, glared at both of them.

'I don't know why you all assume I'm in trouble. Just maybe he wants to say we're doing a good job!'

'Oh, yeah?' the others chorused. 'That'd be likely!'

But no amount of guessing could have prepared her for what Mac actually had to say. Amelia had been sufficiently disturbed by the summons to knock before entering.

'Oh, for heaven's sake, come in, Peterson,' Mac

growled. 'Since when did you knock before barging in here?'

'I'm not barging in,' Amelia countered sharply. 'I was *ordered* to appear. No doubt, so you could yell at me for something more relevant to work than knocking on your door.'

Mac scowled at her.

'How the hell did this start off as an argument?' he demanded. He ran his fingers through his hair and Amelia couldn't help remembering how silky soft it had been. 'Sit down, Peterson. I need to talk to you.'

His voice was gruff—almost desperate. But perhaps she was imagining that because her own inner tension had a fine edge of desperation itself. Working with Mac after what had happened nearly a fortnight earlier was driving her to distraction.

If only it hadn't been so good...

Knees weakening at the thought, Amelia sat.

And waited.

'Well?' Mac eventually said, and Amelia, thinking maybe she'd missed something while immersed in her own wayward and highly censorable thoughts, looked questioningly at him.

'You haven't asked me anything,' she eventually managed when it seemed Mac had been struck dumb.

'I know, but it's not easy,' he complained. 'I've tried to think of ways to say it that don't sound bad, but I can't. The thing is, Peterson, since that night—you know the one I mean—well, I can't help thinking how good things were between us and I wondered if you felt the same and how you'd feel about kind of regular contacts like it.'

Amelia frowned at him as she tried to make sense of this garbled sentence.

PRACTISING AND PREGNANT

**Dedicated doctors, determinedly single—
and unexpectedly pregnant.**

These dedicated doctors have one goal in life—to heal
patients and save lives. They've little time for love, but
somehow it finds them. When they're faced with single
parenthood, too, how do they juggle the demands and
dilemmas of their professional and private lives?

PRACTISING AND PREGNANT

Emotionally entangled stories of doctors in love
from Mills & Boon® Medical Romance™.

'"Kind of regular contacts"?' she repeated faintly. 'Are you suggesting we start going out together?'

It didn't seem likely but, whichever way she considered it, that's how it had sounded to her.

'Good heavens, no,' Mac said, promptly disabusing her of that idea. 'Not a relationship. I'm no good at relationships, I told you that. But getting together every now and then…'

'Physically? As in sex? You're suggesting you pop over to my apartment now and then for a quick—' She couldn't think of a polite word that covered this unbelievable suggestion but fortunately Mac had cut in anyway.

'No, no, nothing like that. I mean, we enjoyed the dinner, too, didn't we? So I thought dinner as well…'

If the original bizarre suggestion had caused small flutters of excitement, this new embroidered version of it spurred anger to life.

'Like payment for what comes after! What do you think I am? How could you possibly suggest such a thing? Get lost, Mac. Go bother someone else. I'm sure there are plenty of women willing to satisfy your libido for the price of a decent dinner, but I don't happen to be one of them.'

'Oh, for Pete's sake, Peterson, you know damn well that isn't what I mean!' Mac exploded, but Amelia ignored him.

She stood up and strode out of the room, with his roar of indignation continuing behind her.

Furious both with Mac and with her physical self for being even slightly interested in his suggestion, she stormed down the corridor, grabbed her jacket and handbag from her locker, then headed for the car park.

'This your car?'

A security man was standing by her vehicle, his badge

glinting in the light shed by a nearby bank of security lights.

'Yes, what's up?' Leftover anger made the question an abrupt demand.

'I heard your anti-theft alarm going and came over in time to chase a couple of young lads away. But not before they'd shoved their screwdrivers into your tyres, Nurse.'

'Screwdrivers?' Amelia echoed, bending down to confirm her two passenger side tyres were as flat as the first glance had suggested.

'It's what kids carry these days. They can break the locks on cars with them. See.'

He pointed to the lock on the passenger door, where a deep indentation had made using a key impossible.

'Damn and blast the little horrors!' Amanda muttered. 'I guess I'll have to call the automobile people.'

'Have you got two spares?' the security man asked, and Amelia fought back the urge to snap at him again. Who on earth carried two spare tyres for driving around the city?

She made do with a head shake and dug in her handbag for her mobile, then her wallet to find the card for the roadside emergency service number.

'They can take it away, then—leave it at a garage where both the tyres and the door lock can be fixed.'

Amelia nodded acceptance of the man's summing-up and made the phone call, then unlocked the driver's-side door and sat in the car until the tow truck arrived.

Half an hour later, with her precious car secured on the back of the truck, she was tossing up whether to return to the hospital, where she knew she'd find a cab, or try hailing one on the street, when a voice called from behind the next row of cars.

'Need a lift?'

It had to be Mac who'd discovered her predicament!

He'd come closer now, emerging from behind a big four-wheel drive to stand beside her and watch the truck disappear.

'No, I'll get a cab,' she said, because standing next to Mac made her wonder if she'd been mad to refuse his earlier offer. Maybe a little of Mac would be better than nothing.

'Don't be stupid, Peterson,' he said, slinging his arm casually around her shoulders. 'You mightn't want to sleep with me, but we're still colleagues so we have to get past all that. It's just that I enjoyed it, and I thought you had, too, and now I keep seeing you naked around the department and it's driving me nuts so I thought I'd say something. We *were* talking about living for the day!'

Amelia was so flummoxed by the 'seeing you naked' bit, she didn't reply, but Mac was apparently unconcerned. He removed his arm from her shoulders to unlock his car, but continued the conversation as calmly as if it were about work or the weather.

'I mean, it would have been stupid if I'd been wanting it and you'd been wanting it and we were both in agonies of self-denial and not knowing it.'

It would, indeed, Amelia thought, climbing into the car to get away from him. And she did want it—but there was no way she was going to get entangled in the kind of casual encounters Mac was suggesting. What if she got fond of him?

Or, heaven forbid, fell in love?

'It's only a lift home,' he said, and she was so startled by his voice interrupting her thoughts she gave an involuntary jerk and turned to stare at him. 'Yet you're sitting there, rammed up against the door and hugging yourself as if I was Jack the Ripper.'

'Don't be stupid,' she retorted. 'You on an ego trip, Mac? Why should I have been thinking about you? I was worrying about my car, if you must know.'

It sounded OK to her and should have put him in his place, but the way his lips slid into a slow, tantalising smile suggested he could see right into her brain and knew she was lying.

Mind you, if he could see through her clothes, maybe he could see into her brain.

If her own brain hadn't been turned into jelly by the smile, she might have been able to strengthen the lie, but it was the kind of smile he'd smiled at her that night— two weeks ago—and it slunk beneath her defences and started the inner dance-circus going again.

'So, are you going to ask me up?'

Once again she was startled but this time by the content of the words, not his voice. She gazed blankly out the window, finally registering they'd pulled up in the visitors' parking lot outside her building.

'I don't think so,' she managed, then realised a firm 'no' would have been much better.

Especially as Mac immediately pounced on the weakness with, 'Take your time deciding. I can wait.'

And although she knew that later she'd think of at least a dozen clever things she should have said in response, the jelly in her head failed to provide a single syllable. She made do with opening the car door, stepping out, then leaning back in to scowl at him, and growl 'Thanks!' in a voice she usually reserved for really irritating telephone salespeople.

But as he drove away, apparently unperturbed by her behaviour, she remembered the smile and felt an inner tremor that suggested an occasional dinner and night in bed with Mac wasn't all that bad an idea.

CHAPTER FIVE

AFTER two more weeks of increasing sexual tension on Amelia's part—Mac seemed totally unperturbed, or perhaps he'd found someone who liked the idea of such a 'no-strings' type of arrangement—she was seriously considering a transfer out of the department.

Purely to get away from him, and so relieve the unremitting turmoil within her body.

But he'd kept his word and had not only raised the issue of a structured career path for A and E nurses, but by some miracle had convinced Enid Biggs of its benefits, so Amelia was now busy, in what free time she had, drawing up a plan to put before the DON.

Free time—that was a joke! Half the department had been struck down by a mystery bug, and she half suspected she'd become the latest victim, but she knew she had to get the plan to Enid before some other project came up and financial considerations might put hers on hold.

So Amelia sat in the little room behind the admissions office, one hand clasped to her queasy stomach, and forced herself to concentrate on the list of courses already on offer within the hospital and at the local university with which St Pat's was associated. Fate intervened before she was halfway through the list, and she was called to an emergency admission.

'Four years old, history of epilepsy, two grand mal seizures both treated by the parents with rectally administered Valium but the child hospitalised afterwards. This time she fitted again on the way in.'

Mac gave Amelia a succinct summing up of the patient as the little girl was wheeled into a cubicle, then he introduced the child's mother, Mrs Carson.

'I'll get a drip in, and I want clonazepam, starting with 0.1 gm, but keep more at hand as I'll increase it if she doesn't stop.'

Amelia produced the drug and dosage he needed, and felt a surge of pride as he calmed the anxious mother while dealing very gently but capably with the child. He talked almost constantly, not in his usual gruff manner but with a gentle assurance that calmed the tense atmosphere and must have eased the mother's nerves.

'It's not working,' he said a little later, when the drug had been increased as far as it was safe to use for the child's weight. 'I've sent for one of our paediatric specialists.'

At that moment, Dan Williams, a paediatric registrar, walked into the cubicle. Mac explained his concerns, and introduced Dan to Mrs Carson.

Dan checked the time drugs had been given, looked at the big clock on the wall then examined the child.

'I'd like to anaesthetise her with a drug that will also paralyse her on a temporary basis so she doesn't continue convulsing,' he told Mrs Carson. 'We'll need to ventilate her, which only means a machine will breathe for her, and this is better done in an intensive-care unit where they have all the necessary equipment for monitoring her condition.'

Mrs Carson nodded, but she looked upset and it was Mac who put his arm around her shoulders.

'Intensive Care always sounds much worse than it is,' he assured her. 'They'll just use machines instead of people to keep an eye on your daughter.'

Amelia was thinking how much she liked this caring

Mac, when her stomach, which had been suggesting it hadn't enjoyed breakfast, finally decided to reject it, and she had to rush from the cubicle, her hand clutched to her mouth, only just making the bathroom before being comprehensively sick.

The nausea passed but she continued to feel wretched.

'I really don't want to pass this bug on to the patients,' she said to Sally, who was on Triage again and allocating nurses to cubicles. 'So keep me out of things unless you get really desperate.'

Fortunately, it didn't happen—the day turning out to be one of those miraculous occasions when no further crisis occurred, and patients were treated and either sent home or admitted like clockwork.

Just as well, Amelia thought to herself as she collected her coat from the locker room and prepared to head home. She was no longer feeling physically sick, but she felt so tired she could have had a little sleep sitting upright in one of the locker room's far from comfortable chairs.

'Ah, Peterson. I hoped I'd catch you. Can I see you in my office for a minute?'

Amelia turned towards Mac, who was looming in the doorway. Her heart jolted in her chest, the dances began in her abdomen and her knees showed an alarming tendency to give way.

But as this was now a familiar reaction to seeing Mac, she managed to ignore it.

'I'm really very tired. Can't it wait until tomorrow?' She hoped she didn't sound as whiny as she felt.

'No!' he said crisply, and he turned away, obviously expecting her to follow, as docile as a lamb.

Which she did—follow, that was. She was feeling far from docile about it, but had decided fighting with him would take more energy than she had right now.

'Sit down,' he said, moving around the desk and dropping into his big office chair.

Amelia sat, surprised to see Mac's desk still relatively paper-free. She was only looking at his desk because it was easier than looking at him, but eventually she had to. To turn her gaze towards his long, rather elegant figure, stretched back in the chair, his hands tucked behind his head—so totally at ease she realised he must have got over the 'seeing her naked' thing.

This made her own ever-increasing awareness of him even more aggravating, so she let a little of it out.

'Well?' she demanded. 'What's so important it couldn't wait until tomorrow?'

Mac studied her for a moment longer, then straightened in his chair, tilting it so he was now leaning slightly forward.

'Are you pregnant?'

For a moment Amelia thought she must have heard wrong, but an echo of the question sounded in her head and disbelief outweighed tiredness.

'Am I pregnant? That's what you wanted to ask? Are you asking all the females in the department? Is it a competition of some kind? Is there a prize?'

Amelia knew she must sound as flabbergasted as she felt, but Mac seemed unperturbed, merely continuing to study her as if she was a case that had intrigued him for some reason.

'You haven't answered,' he pointed out, and she shook her head.

'Of course I'm not pregnant. I've got the bug that's going around, that's all. How the hell could I be pregnant anyway? It's not as if I'm in a relationship. And even if I was pregnant, I don't see what business of yours it would be. Can I go now?'

She felt around for her handbag, which she'd dropped onto the floor when she'd sat down, but, of course, it had hidden itself under the chair. Anxiety made her fumble but she knew she had to get out of the room before she burst into tears. It must be the debilitating effect of the virus, because she almost never cried.

Though she sometimes got a wee bit tearful over not having children, so maybe that was it.

Damn Mac for bringing it up.

She found the bag and stood up, but by now he'd left his chair, come around the desk and was standing there, right beside her. Reaching out his hands towards her—resting them on her shoulders.

She turned to stone under the touch—no, not stone. Stone was cold and she was fiery hot all over.

'Peterson? Amelia?'

It was the sound of her real name on his lips that made her look up—into hazel eyes that had been featuring too often in her dreams. Although now they weren't softened by passion but anxious and concerned. Caring?

'We had unprotected sex four weeks and two days ago—that's how you could be pregnant.'

He said it gently, as if explaining something to a child.

'I know you burbled something at the time—about not being able to conceive so lack of protection not being an issue—but we'd both had too much to drink and were far too aroused by that stage to have thought rationally. Now you're looking downright peaky, and you were sick this morning. How certain are you that you can't conceive? Is there a physical reason it's impossible?'

'"Downright peaky"?' Amelia echoed, twitching away from his hold and glaring furiously at him. 'Well, thanks a lot.'

Mac sighed. 'Trust a bloody woman to pick the one

inessential out of an important conversation and take a man up on it,' he growled. 'If you really want to know, I think you're beautiful—even this morning, when you went that interesting shade of green, I still remembered you as you looked that Saturday night—a fragile, elfin beauty.'

He realised he was now the one right off track and sighed again. 'But that's not the point. Your condition is. How can you be sure you're not pregnant?'

He watched the brown eyes darken and a worried frown draw her finely marked eyebrows together. Unable to resist, he used his forefinger to smooth at the puckered skin and felt a shiver ripple through Peterson's slight body.

'I was married for years and didn't get pregnant,' she said, the velvety eyes looking up into his, perhaps to see if some answer to her uncertainty might be written there. Then she shrugged, as if the physical action could remove all possibilities of pregnancy, and added firmly, 'So of course I'm not now—it's the bug.'

Mac smiled.

'It's the bug, is it? But that's you—Bug. Didn't you tell me your brothers called you that?'

Amelia caught the smile, which softened his deep-set eyes, and felt it twine around her heart, weakening all her resolve and making her tremble with longing for the physical pleasures they'd shared.

'Don't smile at me, Mac,' she whispered, then she did start to cry—not wailing, gut-wrenching crying, just tears sliding down her cheeks.

'Oh, heavens, Peterson. Don't cry!' Mac said, gathering her up against his chest. 'Though maybe it's another symptom of pregnancy, in which case you can't help it. I know my sister got very weepy when she was first pregnant with Petra.'

This conversation didn't make a great deal of sense to Amelia, who was content just to rest her body against Mac's and revel in the feel of his arms around her. She'd fought the attraction she felt for him for a month, and though she knew this was only a temporary cease-fire, she was war-weary and needed to rest.

Then, as the close contact suggested Mac was still interested in the regular encounters he'd suggested, she pushed away, thanked him for his concern and walked out the door.

Mac watched her go and shook his head. He was none the wiser. About how Peterson felt about him—about whether she was pregnant—about anything. How could a conversation he'd planned so carefully have gone so wrong?

He walked back behind his desk and slumped into his chair.

Actually, he *was* wiser about one thing. The attraction he felt towards Peterson was not diminishing with time. If anything, it was growing stronger and stronger, so he had trouble keeping his hands off her—trouble not brushing against her as they worked together or touching her as he passed her in a corridor.

In fact, the problem was growing so strong he wondered if frustration might lead to serious mental or physical problems. Both seemed on the cards!

He stretched out, tucked his hands behind his head and gave the matter some serious thought.

Next morning, unable to face Mac after the weird conversation of the previous evening, and still feeling nauseous and unsettled, Amelia phoned in sick. She spent the day alternately sleeping and worrying. She didn't for a minute entertain Mac's ridiculous pregnancy suggestion—

sure she'd know if such an unlikely thing had happened—but after being held in his arms, if only for comfort, she had to admit that the attraction she felt for him was increasing rather than fading away.

By evening, she'd still failed to find an answer to the problem, though taking Mac up on his suggestion of occasional sex didn't seem as bad an option as it had when he'd suggested it. Bored with her own company, yet not wanting to phone a friend, she was frowning at the lack of interesting viewing on TV and wondering if the local video store delivered when the bell rang, announcing a visitor was standing outside on the ground floor and wanting admission to the building. She crossed to the monitor screen by the front door and saw the back view of a man's head.

Alistair, her oldest brother, invariably stood that way, and Amelia knew he was checking out the landscaping at the entrance to the building. In the family construction company, Alistair was the one with the most interest in the aesthetic appeal of any project the company built.

'Door's open, come on up, Alistair,' she said, pleased to have company but also relieved she didn't have to get out of the housecoat she was wearing.

She opened the front door to her unit so he could come straight in when the lift arrived, then walked through to the kitchen to make a pot of coffee.

'I'm not Alistair but you'd opened the lobby door before I could tell you and I wanted to get in before it shut.'

Mac's voice, unfamiliar in that it sounded vaguely apologetic, stopped her in her tracks.

Telling herself she could handle it—all she had to do was stay calm—she turned, and saw him standing in the middle of her living room.

'I shut your apartment door. I hope that was right.'

There must be something wrong with her ears because now he sounded uncertain, and Mac was never uncertain.

'Anyway,' he continued, perhaps realising she'd been struck dumb as well as turned to stone, 'I brought a test kit and I've got a plan, and I thought we'd find out and if you're not then that's OK, but if you are, I could tell you the plan.'

Dumbfounded didn't begin to cover it. Amelia stared at the man who stood in her living room, holding a small, paper-bagged item out towards her.

With a massive effort, she pulled herself together. She looked around at her familiar surroundings, searching for normal in a world gone crazy.

'I was making coffee. Would you like some?'

Mac nodded, then he frowned.

'If you're pregnant, you shouldn't be drinking coffee.'

The tension inside Amelia snapped, and with it her temper.

'I am not pregnant and even if I was it's none of your business what I drink,' she yelled at him. 'Now, do you want coffee or not?'

He was still looking unfamiliarly uncomfortable, which made her feel even edgier.

'And sit down,' she ordered. 'I can't deal with you standing there like a lost tree.'

He sat, but not before he'd put his package on the dining-room table—halfway between where he'd been and where she was.

Neutral ground?

Amelia turned away, but by now her nerves were so strung out her fingers shook, and even the simplest task of measuring coffee into the machine proved too much for her.

'Let me do it.'

Mac's voice, right behind her, made her jump. Was she in such a state her usually alert senses had failed to register his approach?

He moved her aside, one hand on her shoulder shifting her firmly out of the way, and took over the coffee-making as if it were his kitchen they were in, not hers.

Unable to stay close to him, Amelia stepped away, finding herself by the dining-room table, her eyes drawn, like iron filings to magnets, to the packet on the table.

Of course she couldn't be pregnant.

She pressed her hand to her stomach—thinking of the times she'd pressed it there and ached with regret that it would never swell with pregnancy. But Brad now had a child by his second wife, so the failure hadn't been his.

She shook her head, refusing to allow hope to enter her heart.

'It wouldn't hurt to take the test.'

Mac had started the coffee-machine and was now watching her.

'I'm not pregnant,' she said stubbornly.

'Then prove it.'

She glared at him—something she seemed to have been doing even more of late.

'I don't need to,' she snapped. 'I know!'

But she didn't really know, a traitorous voice inside her pointed out.

'I do!' she told it, realising she'd spoken aloud when Mac grinned at her.

'Sounds more like a marriage vow than a denial,' he teased, and she turned away because a teasing Mac reminded her of what they're shared that night.

'You're like water wearing away at stone,' she said, an hour later, when Mac's unwavering demands had riled her so much she'd grabbed the package and was heading for the bathroom. 'I'll do it, not because I think there's even the remotest possibility but to shut you up because, knowing you, if I don't you'll start asking me at work in front of everyone. Anything to get your own way.'

She strode away, tearing off the wrappings, reading the instructions, then, in the privacy of the bathroom, pulling out the test stick. It was such a simple thing to do she regretted not doing it earlier. It would have stopped Mac nagging and they might have enjoyed their time together. Now, she guessed, she'd have to show him the stick just to prove him wrong.

Prove him wrong?

She looked at it again, blinked, then grabbed the box and reread the instructions.

Then she sat down on the floor of the bathroom because her legs would no longer hold her up.

Mac came in some time later. She'd vaguely heard him call her name, heard him knock and call out again, but it was all far away—in another world perhaps.

'Come on, let's get you off the cold floor.'

Mac was speaking gently, easing his arms around her body, lifting her off the floor as if she were a child.

And he was smiling. She could hear the smile in his voice, and she guessed it was because he'd seen the stick and knew he'd been proved right.

He certainly wouldn't be smiling about her being pregnant, but Mac liked being right.

He carried her into the bedroom, then muttered something about the bed being a danger zone and backed out, taking her into the living room instead and setting her down on the couch.

'Did you faint?'

She frowned at him.

'Of course I didn't faint,' she told him, speaking crossly though she should have been pleased to discover she *could* speak.

He was squatting beside her and now he took hold of her hands.

'I realise this is a shock to you,' he said, and now the smile was on his face as well as in his voice, 'but because I suspected it since you've been feeling ill, I've had a few days to get used to the idea and I've got a plan.'

Amelia stared at him, trying to reconcile this quiet, serious, almost humble Mac with the grouchy, unobliging autocrat she'd known for years at work.

'A plan? Why do *you* need a plan?'

He squeezed her hands.

'Not me, us,' he corrected. 'And we need it for your pregnancy.' He paused then frowned, but not angrily, more as if he was having trouble finding the words he needed.

'That's if you decide to go through with it, which is entirely up to you, of course, because you're the one who'll be inconvenienced, but I thought if I put my side of it to you, it might help you come to a decision.'

He paused, studying her face as if to see if she'd followed him this far.

She had, and her hand had crept protectively to her stomach when he'd suggested the next decision would be hers.

'The thing is, Peterson…' he went on—apparently satisfied by what he saw in her face. 'And if you laugh, or mention this to anyone in the entire world, I'll kill you, but since my sister had her baby recently I've been kind of thinking that I wouldn't mind having one myself. Of course, that was the last thing on my mind that night we— well, you know what we did, and it certainly wasn't to get you pregnant, heaven forbid. But since it's happened, Peterson, and I'd really kind of like to have a child, well, my plan was that I'd keep you through your pregnancy so you don't have to work if you don't want to, and I'll pay all the expenses—doctors, clothing, furniture and the lot—and if you don't want the child when it arrives, I'll assume full responsibility. Get a nanny, of course, but still be a good father. I know it's bad timing for you, with the new work project you've got in hand, which is why I want to do whatever I can to help.'

The flow of words and garbled information finally ceased. Amelia felt as if she'd absorbed maybe an eighth of it, and that eighth didn't make much sense.

Although one bit stuck out—holding, as it did, memories of another offer Mac had made.

'You'll pay me to have this baby? Like some surrogate mother? What do you think I am, Mac? A human test-tube? A convenient womb?'

'No, no—'

But before he could get into the meat of his protest, Amelia had found more to anger her.

'And just because you've gone clucky—which is something men have laughed at women about for years—this is suddenly *your* baby. What if I don't want a nanny?'

Mac rubbed his fingers along her forearm, causing panic in the fine hairs over which they brushed.

'I don't think we need to decide about a nanny right now,' he said gently. 'I know I mightn't have made much sense, but what I was trying to say is that I wouldn't mind having this baby—though you'd physically have to have it, of course—but I'll be there for you, in any way you want me to be.'

He leant forward, and kissed her very gently on the lips. It was more a promise than a real kiss, but it awoke the aching hunger Amelia had felt all month, and it was only with difficulty she restrained her hands from reaching out and pulling him closer—kissing him back with the passion his salute had lacked.

Mac eased back onto his heels, putting space between them because that kiss, though only the most fleeting of caresses, had reignited the desire he'd felt since entering her apartment. She'd been walking away from him but, seeing her small, slim figure, clad only in a satiny gown, with the dark, lustrous hair she usually confined so ruthlessly flowing down her back, had put his manhood on full alert.

It was the hair—he was certain of it. The dark shiny brown tresses, shot through with red and gold, tantalised him, urging him to thread his fingers into it and use it to draw her closer to his body, to entangle her so they were intertwined.

He touched it now, smoothing it back from her face, warning his fingers not to linger, though they took no notice.

She looked so small—so fragile—curled up, half sitting, half lying on the big leather sofa. And the dazed look in her brown eyes revealed she was still shocked by her discovery—so much so he couldn't bring himself to leave her.

But if he stayed…

'We'll work it out,' he said gently. 'When you've had time to think things through, we'll talk it through. There's no rush to decide anything, Amelia. Right now you have to think of yourself and concentrate on staying well.'

Mac continued to stroke her hair and saw her eyelids grow heavy, then, within minutes, she was breathing the steady, shallow breath of sleep.

Mac shifted off his haunches—his thighs and calves

had been protesting for ages—and settled into a chair across from her, an unfamiliar protectiveness swamping him.

He had a number of options, he decided. He could leave Amelia sleeping where she was.

He could carry her into the bedroom, where he now felt he was sufficiently in control of things to settle her into bed without throwing himself in with her.

He could go home.

He studied her for a moment and decided leaving her on her own wasn't an option.

In the end, he carried her into her room, enjoying the weight of her in his arms, the feel of her sleep-heavy body snuggled against his chest. Taking care not to wake her, he straightened the gown around the body that had haunted him for a month, then covered her with the sheet and cotton blanket, tucking them in around her so she was held securely in the bed.

'I can't believe I'm doing this, Peterson,' he said quietly to the sleeping figure. 'Not when the one thing on my mind for the past month has been to be tucked in there with you—with my arms, not a damn sheet, holding you securely.'

He then explored the flat, found the spare bedroom with a queen-sized bed already made up and returned to the living room. At least, after last time he knew where to find a pen and paper. He wrote a note, explaining he was staying in the spare bedroom in case she needed someone, then tiptoed back into her bedroom where, with only a small touch to the shining hair, he left the note where he'd left the last one.

Not that she appreciated his concern. Oh, no! Not Peterson.

He'd set his internal alarm to wake at six so he'd have

time to get back to his place and have a shower and shave before work, but for some reason it didn't work and he woke to the sound of a furious banging on the already open bedroom door.

'You didn't set my alarm clock!' the noise-maker accused, poking a tousled head around the doorjamb. 'And unless you came prepared to stay the night, you're going to be late for work as well.'

Either sleep or anger had stained her cheeks a rosy pink, and with the tangled mass of dark hair around her flushed face she looked like a flustered angel.

Mac smiled at her, though a quick glance at his watch had told him she was right and he had no time at all for fanciful metaphors or smiles. He shoved off the covers and stood up, only realising he was naked when the colour deepened in Peterson's cheeks and she beat a hasty retreat.

'It's not as if she's seeing anything she hadn't seen before,' he grumbled to himself as he pulled on his clothes and did a mental calculation of how long it would take him to get home then back to the hospital.

He would be late for work, no doubt about it. But he kept a change of clothes in his locker and an electric razor in a drawer of his desk. If he went straight to the hospital, he'd be early, not late.

Perhaps he could buy Peterson breakfast somewhere on the way.

He studied the bed, not wanting to leave it unmade yet uncertain about stripping it. In the end, he made it—a task made difficult by the slippery bedcover that kept sliding off to one side or the other. Finally satisfied, he left the room to find a very different Peterson emerging from her bedroom.

The hair was slicked back in its bunched arrangement, her uniform shirt was crisply pressed but hanging out over the skirt she wore so it only hinted at the shapely body beneath it.

'How about I buy us breakfast somewhere on the way to work?' he suggested, his good mood restored by the fact that his eyes seemed to have retained their X-ray vision where Peterson's body was concerned.

'Breakfast?'

She said the word in much the same way someone offered ptomaine poisoning might repeat the suggestion. 'I'm throwing up every morning and you're suggesting breakfast.'

'You should eat something—it helps with morning sickness.'

The brown eyes fired darts of loathing.

'You'd know, of course,' she said.

'Well, I would!' Mac stood his ground. 'Charlotte—that's my sister—had terrible morning sickness, and I asked every O and G fellow in the hospital for advice and the only thing they all came up with was small meals and often. You should actually have a cup of tea and a dry biscuit before you get out of bed—Charlotte found that helped.'

'And how do I achieve this wonder cure without getting out of bed?' Scathing didn't begin to describe the tone. 'Teleport?'

'I could do it,' Mac heard himself offer. 'I mean, if it helped and made you feel better. I meant it when I said I'd do whatever I could, Peterson, if you want to have this baby. That means from right now. I could shift in, sleep in the spare room if that's what you want—whatever helps, Peterson.'

Amelia looked startled, then shocked, then despairing—each emotion chasing across her face as clear to read as block printing.

'Oh, Mac!' she whispered, and the dark eyes filmed. 'What are we going to do?'

Mac felt something shift in his chest—but he'd been told so often he didn't have a heart, not an emotional one, it couldn't have been that. He covered his momentary confusion by reaching out and pulling Peterson into his arms, tucking her body close to his.

'We'll start with breakfast. I know a place that has a variety of breads and pastries, and great teas and coffees. There's sure to be something there to settle a nauseous stomach.'

He eased her away so he could tilt her face up and look into her eyes.

'And after that we'll simply take it one step at a time. Whatever you want to do and however you want to do it. OK?'

Amelia straightened in his arms and smiled, then drew away and laughed.

'Oh, dear, I wish I'd taped that, Mac,' she said, still laughing. 'The moment I decide on something that doesn't fit in with your grand plans, you'll be ordering me around the way you always do.'

'I will not,' Mac retorted, but he was pleased to see the old argumentative Peterson had resurfaced. The wan, uncertain Peterson had been affecting him in strange ways and making him feel a macho protectiveness which he knew the real Peterson would regard as a source of vast amusement and endless mockery.

CHAPTER SIX

THOUGH there was no way she was going to admit it to Mac, Amelia did feel better after a cup of a strange flavoured tea, recommended by the proprietor of the café Mac suggested, and a small, but delicious, seeded bagel, spread with a morsel of cream cheese and a sprinkling of sultanas.

So, by the time she arrived at work, physically she was fine, though mentally she was a write-off. If her brain had been like jelly the previous week, today it was filled with cotton wool. She was aware that she needed to think about the situation—*really* needed to think about it—but the woolly fluff in her head prevented anything but the most basic of messages getting through.

She just hoped the work-oriented part was still functioning, a hope confirmed with her first patient, a small boy who'd somehow lodged a watch battery in his ear.

Sam Watson, aged three, was relatively subdued—or perhaps overawed by the hospital atmosphere. First he'd had to sit in the cavernous waiting room with a lot of noisy strangers, then he'd been taken into a small, poky little room, where a lot of strange paraphernalia would have worried even the bravest of children.

'Children seem to feel obliged to stuff things in the holes they find around their head,' Amelia said to his mother—who seemed long-suffering rather than concerned. Amelia settled Sam on an examination table, found a mirror and magnifying eyeglasses, and, explaining what she was doing to both child and mother, peered into the small opening.

'It's lodged in the outer ear canal and there's no sign of the tympanic membrane being punctured,' she said, hearing someone enter the room behind her and assuming it was Rick Stewart, the registrar on her team today.

'So we'll try syringing it out first,' a deep voice said, and at the same time a hand brushed across her arm, startling her body into awareness.

'Is the department so short-staffed you're working on non-urgent cases?' she asked Mac, handing him the head mirror and turning away to get a syringe and saline to flush the ear.

'No, but my office wasn't very appealing and, besides…' he flashed one of his rare but ravishing smiles at Mrs Watson '…ears are my special love.'

Amelia shivered, remembering how Mac had tantalised her with little nips and nibbles on her ear lobes on that one momentous night. She glanced his way and saw a little twist of the smile had remained on his lips, and guessed he'd said it deliberately.

'But, looking at this one, I don't think a syringe will shift it. Would you get an angled probe for me, please, Sister?'

'Oh, so polite, Mac?' Amelia murmured at him, but she found the probe he wanted—one with a curved end which could be slid in over the foreign object and used to pull it out.

'We use this,' Mac said, showing it to the patient and his mother but addressing the information to the parent, 'because tweezers might push the object further in. Though your mum won't need to know that, will she, Sam, because you won't ever do this again, will you?'

The child looked up at him with fearful blue eyes.

'It won't hurt,' Amelia assured Sam, taking his hand as Mac bent over the little boy.

But she was no longer thinking of either Sam or Mac. Seeing those eyes had triggered something inside her, had somehow confirmed the fact that her child—hers and Mac's—was right now becoming more than just a cluster of cells, or a rather scary thought.

It was a reality—she was pregnant—and in eight months or so she'd have a child.

A swear word she kept for really desperate occasions fluttered through her lips, but it was more wondering than desperate or despairing—her reaction more miraculously amazed than distressed.

Mac's whispered, 'No swearing in front of the patients,' told her he'd heard, but Mrs Watson, who was lifting Sam off the table and talking reassuringly to him, didn't appear to have noticed anything amiss.

'Something bothering you?' Mac asked, trapping Amelia in the cubicle when the pair had departed.

Amelia looked at him and shook her head.

'It's just getting through to me,' she said, the wonderment causing the head shaking to continue. 'That I'm pregnant. That I'm going to have a baby.'

Mac held his hand against her cheek.

'That *we're* going to have a baby. Our baby,' he said firmly.

Amelia stopped shaking her head, but wasn't up to nodding just yet.

'I think I need to get used to my side of things first, Mac,' she said. 'There are so many implications—so many things to consider.'

'Dr McDougal to Emergency Admissions—Dr McDougal, Emergency Admissions.'

'Take your time,' he said, then added a warning. 'But not too much.'

He touched her lightly on the shoulder and walked away, and Amelia pressed her hand against her cheek, feeling the warmth where his palm had been.

Not too much, he'd said. The way she felt now, if she had the gestation period of an elephant, she still wouldn't be ready for the implications of it being 'our' baby when the 'our' in question was herself and Mac.

Or had he said 'not too much' because if she decided to terminate the pregnancy then the sooner she did it the better?

For all his assurances that he'd like to have a baby, all his talk about paying the expenses because he really wanted a child, was he hoping she'd decide not to go through with it?

Once again she found her hand resting on her stomach. One thing she knew for sure. Not going through it just wasn't an option. She'd wanted a baby from the time she'd married Brad, but in recent years it had seemed like an impossible dream.

No, fate might possibly intervene, but there was no way she would do anything to not have this baby.

She sighed, but a sense of well-being and excitement flooded through her, as if her body was telling her she'd made the right decision.

For her.

But was it the right decision for Mac? And what would be the implications of having Mac's baby?

Somehow, she'd have to find out.

'The problem is, Mac,' she said, when he'd found her, two hours after her normal finishing time, in the little office behind the admissions desk, where she was putting the finishing touches to a suggested list of courses for A and E nursing staff, 'it's not just a matter of deciding whether or not to have the baby—it's all the implications of it. For a start, there are all that lot out there. How would we handle them?'

Amelia waved her hand to where the normal hustle and bustle of the department was continuing, with conversation, occasional shouts for help or equipment and the odd bit of gossip floating in the air.

'I mean, I can't keep a pregnancy hidden for ever—I'm not the right shape for a start—and then when the staff realise it's yours, well, yours and mine...' The sentence died, Amelia unable to voice the enormity of the impact their news would have.

'They'll handle it,' Mac said stoutly, but he didn't sound all that stout. In fact, he sounded startled, as if the thought hadn't occurred to him—while the frown accompanying his words also gave the lie to his statement.

'They'll have a ball is what you mean,' Amelia told him. 'It will be the talk of the hospital and, what's worse, they'll think you and I have something going—that we're in a relationship, that we're a couple...'

She looked at him, trying to read his face. He was still frowning. If anything, the frown had deepened, and apparently she'd caused that increase in indentation as it was directed at her.

'Would that be so totally disastrous, Peterson?' he demanded. 'Not the gossip—that's nothing. It lasts a day or two, a week at most, then something else comes up and takes its place.'

He waved his hand to dismiss the gossip as negligible, then continued, 'But the couple thing. I mean, I'd kind of already suggested it earlier and you got all huffy, but now,

with a baby on the way—if that's what happens—
wouldn't being a couple be the best way to handle it?'

'I had every right to get huffy! What you "kind of
suggested" was anything but a relationship, if I remember
rightly,' she reminded him. 'It was more a series of one-
night stands, because you were, as you pointed out, hopeless at relationships.'

'But this would be different. I'm talking marriage here,
Peterson. I think that's the right thing for the baby.' Mac
made it sound as if even a two-year-old should understand. 'On top of that, we know each other pretty well,
and we did enjoy the physical side of things that night,
so what could be a better basis for a marriage?'

Amelia realised there was absolutely no point in men-
tioning the 'L' word. She'd seen enough of Mac's reac-
tions to other members of the staff foolish enough to de-
clare their love for each other in his hearing to know it
wasn't in his vocabulary.

'So that's all you want out of marriage—sex and the
baby?'

He looked startled but recovered well, growling at her
about women always taking things the wrong way, and
how they'd always been friends so they'd have friendship—companionship—going for them as well.

And that's as good as it's going to get, Amelia realised,
battling a ridiculous sense of disappointment.

'Anyway,' he continued briskly, as if there was no more
to be said on the subject of relationships, 'we don't have
to rush but we do have a lot to sort out. You have to think
about the wedding. Considerations like family come into
it. I assume those brothers of yours would eventually notice a pregnancy. And even if they didn't, mothers tend
to catch on quite quickly when their daughter starts growing a bump where one hasn't been before.'

Amelia repeated the swear word she'd used earlier, but with considerably more force. Her brothers? Her mother? And what about Dad?

'How the hell am I going to tell *them*?' she muttered, to herself, not Mac, though naturally he heard, and with the un-Mac-like generosity he was displaying in this situation he leapt in with yet another plan.

'I'll do it for you. You can take me to visit, and I'll tell them how I've lusted after you for years then finally you saw the error of your ways and decided to accept my suit, and we're getting married and having a baby.'

He spread his arms, as if expecting applause for this absolutely, utterly, totally and comprehensively ridiculous solution.

Amelia's mind had caught the least important bit and, instead of applauding, she asked, 'Have you?'

His puzzled look told her he didn't understand so she elaborated.

'Lusted after me for years?'

Momentarily taken aback, he hesitated, giving Amelia time to answer for him.

'Of course you haven't, and, anyway, I think lust would be the wrong word to use with my parents—not that we're going to do anything like that.'

Mac smiled at her, and the little buzz of attraction which now was a permanent feature in her body whenever she was near him became a big buzz.

'Adored you from afar?' he offered. 'And don't be silly. Of course we'll tackle your family together. It'll be a quid pro quo thing, Peterson, because I sure as hell will need you with me when I tell mine.'

Amelia frowned severely at him.

'Bad choice of words, Mac,' she said. 'If I remember

rightly, and I do, it was one of your "quid pro quo" things that got us into this.'

Mac chuckled, a sound so unexpected it spread its warmth through Amelia's blood and started messages of need deep down in the innermost part of her body.

Dangerous messages of need!

Not good when she knew in her heart of hearts a marriage based on sex and a baby wouldn't work for her.

She pushed the chair back, which brought her closer to where he was perched on the side of the desk so their conversation couldn't be overheard by anyone in the outer office.

'I've got to go,' she told him.

Unfortunately, her efforts to back away from him tipped the chair over, and she'd have followed it if he hadn't caught her by the shoulder.

Mac didn't speak, but the surprise in his eyes suggested he, too, had felt the surge of awareness that had jolted through her body.

'Not here,' she murmured as his hand gently tugged her closer.

Shock replaced the surprise in his eyes, then a gleam of something that went further than amusement lit the hazel depths.

'I came in to offer you a lift. I drove you to work, remember.'

With a mouth suddenly too dry for speech, Amelia nodded. She knew exactly where the unspoken part of this conversation was leading and honesty compelled her to admit, if only to herself, that it was what she wanted.

Mac took her arm and led her out past the two women in the outer office. Neither took much notice, though one called something to Mac.

He kept walking, but fate caught up with them as they

passed the curtained cubicles in the emergency admissions area.

'Mac, thank goodness you're still here. Paul Curry's just fainted and I've told him to go home, and the intern on this shift is already off with flu. I've a child choking in four, and an ambulance on its way with the first of the victims from a multi-vehicle accident.'

Loris Quinn, senior doctor on duty on the evening shift, managed to convey all this information in a very short time, then, as Mac strode off to attend to the child, she seemed to recognise Amelia.

'I don't suppose you could stay as well,' she said. 'Half the nursing staff have got this bug, and we're so short-handed I don't know how we'll handle the accident victims.'

'One by one,' Amelia reminded her. 'At least they should be tagged by the time they get here. And of course I'll stay, but I'll check with Susie first that she's put out an SOS for extra nursing staff. A and E should never be left short-handed.'

She dashed away, checking in first with Susie McLeod who was senior nurse this shift. Susie confirmed help had been requested, though it was doubtful they'd get it as the entire hospital seemed to be suffering from the virus.

'If you could stay just an hour or so,' Susie said to her, as the 'whoop-whoop' of an ambulance siren announced it had arrived. 'You might take this first patient.'

Amelia nodded and joined a couple of porters outside the emergency entrance. The ambulance had stopped and the attendants were already wheeling out the first patient. His eyes were open and the green tag attached to his leg told Amelia he was priority three—treatment could be delayed if others needed help before him. Priorities one and two—immediate and urgent respectively—often came in later, because the paramedics had to stabilise them at the scene before transporting them.

Amelia took the sheet of information already gathered about the patient from the attendant, and the porters wheeled him inside. She directed them to an open cubicle at the end of the room, then turned as a second patient was unloaded from the ambulance. Her tag was also green, but she was obviously pregnant, and Amelia, conscious of the risk of any accident to an unborn baby, crossed to the phone and put out a call for an O and G registrar to report to A and E.

Susie came out of cubicle four and took charge of the woman, directing Amelia back to the cubicle where the man had been taken. Once there, she spoke to him, asking what had happened, checking vital signs at the same time, moving, watching, listening. A young doctor she didn't know appeared, examined the patient and ordered X-rays, then, as the man was being wheeled away, another ambulance arrived.

'Come with me—we'll take this one,' the doctor, whose ID proclaimed him to be Dean Richards, said.

Amelia followed him out to the ambulance bay. It was the beginning of a few hours of organised chaos. Cries for tests, blood, plasma, saline and instruments were going up from all the cubicles and echoing back from the walls. Voices cursed and shouted, nurses ran between the curtained alcoves, delivering whatever was required, fuming at impatient orders but carrying them out in any case.

'What the hell are you still doing here?'

The department had returned to normal and Amelia was leaning against the wall in the corridor, wondering where she'd find the strength to walk out the front entrance and lift her arm high enough to wave down a taxi. She opened her eyes and looked up into Mac's glowering face.

'Same thing as you, I suppose,' she told him. 'Responding to an emergency.'

'They could have coped without you.' The words grated harshly from his lips. 'In your condition you should be looking after yourself, not working here until you're practically fainting from exhaustion.'

'And who appointed you my keeper?' Amelia demanded, so angry with his attitude her hands clenched into fists and she wanted to batter them against his chest.

Not that they'd have done much good—like a flea bashing an elephant.

'I did,' he said, stepping towards her, his hands reaching out so for a moment she thought he was going to lift her into his arms again.

In the hospital?

She ducked away, but wasn't fast enough to escape his hand, which latched itself around her shoulders and drew her close.

'Get used to it, Peterson,' he growled, bending low so she couldn't miss either the words or the intonation. 'That's my baby you're carrying in there and, though I'm willing to give you time to come to terms with it and let you do things your way, eventually every damn worker in this hospital is going to know it.'

The pride in his voice made Amelia's knees feel so weak she almost, but not quite, forgot the buzzing in the rest of her body.

Mac drove her home, ignored her assurances she could make it up to her apartment without an escort, but left her at the front door.

'Make sure you have something to eat as soon as you get up. Better still, how about I come around in the morning and take you to the same place for breakfast? You said the tea agreed with you.'

Amelia studied him for a moment.

'You haven't had a personality transplant, have you, Mac?'

'Sarcasm is the lowest form of wit, Peterson,' he growled, then he touched her cheek. 'But you're too tired for me to be arguing with you. Go to bed.'

He bent his head and brushed his lips against hers.

'Goodnight.'

Dazed by the kiss, she propped herself against the door as two long strides took him back to the lift. He pressed the button, then turned back to her, digging through his pockets and finally producing a crumpled piece of paper from one of them and a pen from the other.

He scribbled something as the lift arrived and the doors slid open. He stuck his foot in the opening to hold them ajar, crumpled the paper even more and threw it across to her.

'My phone number and mobile and pager number, Peterson. If you need me for anything at all, from a cup of tea to a hug, you make sure you call.'

He waggled his fingers at her in a most un-Mac-like manner, then the doors slid closed. Amelia straightened out the piece of paper and read the numbers.

Would she ever feel the need to call any of them?

She thought of the times when she'd longed for a man's comforting hug—from someone other than one of her brothers—and shook her head, considering the dangers of hugging Mac. Then idly, to distract her mind as much as for any other reason, she turned the piece of paper over.

It was a receipt for dinner for two at Capriccio's—not for the night she'd been his partner but, according to the date in the top right-hand corner, for the Tuesday after he'd made his offer of a 'dinner-and-sex' arrangement between them.

'It didn't take you long to find a replacement,' she muttered at the departed guest. 'Just four short days!' She crumpled the paper in her tightening fist and flung it hard against the wall.

Then she retrieved it, and carefully straightened it out again. If ever there was an omen, this was it. Mac could talk all he liked about marriage—because he considered it the best option for a child he undoubtedly wanted—but marriage without love didn't work. Not for her! She'd found that out with Brad, when she'd realised she'd mistaken attraction and friendship for a deeper emotion.

Mac might want this baby—the pride in his voice when he'd spoken earlier had confirmed that fact. So it was only fair he had some involvement. Also, it would be good for the child to know its father. But to live with Mac—with anyone—in a loveless marriage?

No way would that be happening.

She'd go it alone—well, she and the baby, there'd be two of them—and first thing tomorrow morning, she'd tell him.

Mac drove away from the building feeling curiously flat.

Tiredness, he told himself. It's been a long day—a long couple of days.

But this rationalisation failed to reassure him, especially as the excitement he'd felt since realising Peterson might be pregnant had been damped down by this new sensation.

He frowned into the night, irritated by the fact that he couldn't pinpoint the cause of his gloom. He prided himself on his self-knowledge and was the first to admit to his flaws and faults, so where did this flatness come from?

From the fact you're driving home when you'd rather be in Peterson's flat?

The question, hitting him out of nowhere, shocked him

into braking suddenly, causing the car behind him to blast a reprimand. It was a timely reminder, he told himself. Forget your mood and concentrate on driving. Most of the people heading out of the city at this time of night have been out enjoying themselves—probably having a drink or two—so you have to be alert, not lost in non-productive conjecture.

He swung onto the entrance to the motorway which would take him out of the city towards his suburban town-house and accelerated up the sharp curve of the on-ramp. At first the sudden blaze of light confused him, while the noise of sirens echoed in his head.

Then the lights went out.

CHAPTER SEVEN

AMELIA paced the floor of her living room. Surely Mac had said he'd pick her up and take her to breakfast—and he certainly didn't know how furious the receipt had made her. Or anything of the decision it had helped her make.

So where was he?

Backing out of the marriage situation—that's where!

He'd been kind the previous night—and the night before that—but out of sight was obviously out of mind with Mac, and he'd forgotten.

Well, that suited her just fine!

Tired of waiting, and increasingly nauseous, she made her own cup of tea and nibbled at a piece of dry toast, neither of which improved either her restless stomach or her temper.

'Heard about Mac?'

Sally asked the question as Amelia walked into the locker room—late—to dump her handbag.

Possibilities flashed through her mind. He was leaving, applying to be an astronaut—that should take him far enough away from her...

'Heard what?' she asked, hoping it had only been seconds not hours since Sally had spoken.

'He was in a car accident last night. It was on this morning's news, although they didn't mention his name. A stolen car involved in a police chase crossed the median strip and came down the on-ramp as he was going up. He must have had a hot date that he was driving home from the city, not the hospital.'

Amelia stood very still, certain all the physical functioning of her body had halted. She drew in air so she could form words to ask the question, then found she didn't dare let the thought escape her lips lest the horror of it overwhelm her.

Fortunately, Sally continued.

'He's up in ICU. They're saying semi-coma, but who knows with head injury, especially an acceleration-deceleration injury?'

Amelia's brain had obviously started working again as it obligingly threw up a plethora of terrible information about such injuries, even an illustration of how they occurred—when the sudden cessation of forward movement threw the soft mass of the brain forward against the bony plates in the front of the skull, then slammed it back again against the hard bones at the rear.

'So we're a doctor short, though we've got an extra intern replacing Rick who's off sick, and we'll probably be a few nurses short as well.'

Amelia realised that was good. The busier she was, the less time she'd have to worry. She locked her bag away, pulled on a clean pink coverall and followed Sally out of the room.

But being busy didn't stop her thinking—not entirely.

Where did she stand with Mac? Did one night of intimacy and a pregnancy entitle her to visiting time in the ICU?

She knew damn well it didn't, but that didn't stop a feeling of urgency that she *should* be there, talking to him, touching him, reminding him about the baby—telling him he had to stay alive for the baby if nothing else.

Because, if Mac should die, her child would be fatherless.

It was one thing to decide against marriage, but her child needed a father, so Mac would have to live.

Having made this decision, she felt a lot better, and better still when, during a lull in the influx of patients, she had time to phone the ICU. By sheer luck she found Rachel Reynolds on duty. She and Rachel had trained together and remained friends, although they rarely caught up with each other.

'He's OK,' Rachel told her. 'Well, as OK as you can get with head injury. Contusions and lacerations of the brain but no sign of any more dangerous developments as yet. He's been classified as semi-coma—responding to painful stimuli but not verbal questions or commands.'

'I've always thought that "responding to painful stimuli" was a terrible way to classify a patient—I mean, I respond to painful stimuli when I'm fully conscious.'

'I know,' Rachel agreed, 'but until we come up with something better…'

'Can I visit?'

As soon as the question was out Amelia knew it had been a mistake, but she'd had to ask.

'Why? Something going on between the two of you? I haven't heard it on the gossip line so you must have kept it quiet.'

'You haven't heard it because nothing's happening,' Amelia snapped. 'But we've been colleagues for a long time and he did me a favour recently.' She hesitated, then added, 'I care about him, Rache.'

'About Mac? The ogre of A and E? We *are* talking about the same person?'

'Shouldn't you be checking your monitors or something?' Amelia said crossly, then she slammed down the phone.

Somehow she got through the day, but when she finished her shift, instead of heading home, she made her way down to the library. The texts she found on head injuries were hardly reassuring, though one kindly author had drawn a graph of a patient's progress up from coma, semi-coma, to stupor, then confusion and finally alertness. This man contended it usually happened that way, providing no further setbacks such as meningitis, lung infections, haematomas or other horrifyingly ominous complications occurred.

At the stupor level, the next step up, if Rachel's explanation of his condition was correct, he could be roused with difficulty but would probably respond to simple questions.

Were there ever any simple questions? she wondered, returning the books to the shelves then making her way up to the ICU.

Her uniform meant no one stopped her walking into the intensive-care unit, and the sister on duty behind the bank of monitors seemed to think it was natural she'd want to check on a colleague.

'He's in four,' she said, nodding towards a window opposite the nurses' station. 'That's his mother in there now. His sister came up earlier and brought her baby, thinking he might respond to her. Apparently he's mad about the child, but it didn't help.'

Amelia felt her heart clench with pain. She thanked the woman and crossed the room, looking through the window at the man who lay so still.

'Mac!' she whispered helplessly, realising, when she saw the craggy profile with its stubborn jutting chin, that she might be just the teensiest, tiniest bit in love with him.

With Mac? her head scoffed, and as the woman sitting by the bed, perhaps sensing her presence, turned, Amelia walked away.

Of course she couldn't be in love with Mac. The heavy lump of misery in her chest was because of the baby, not Mac. And the strung-out feeling in her nerves and the tension in her muscles were caused by the fact her baby might lose his or her father, not because she might lose Mac.

After all, he wasn't hers to lose.

Five long anxiety-filled days later, Rachel finally had something good to report.

'He's awake some of the time but confused and disoriented,' she said. 'Apparently he thinks Petra is his baby, though he's calling her something more like Peter, and he seems terribly anxious about her. Doug Blake, the neurologist who's in charge of him, is concerned about the confusion and the distress it's causing. He feels if the family can't somehow reassure him, he might have to put him into an induced coma for a while and bring him out of it more slowly.'

Neurologists often treated their head-injured patients by inducing a coma, Amelia reminded herself, but it didn't help the worry knotting her gut and straining her nerves to snapping point.

She thought through what Rachel had said and brooded on possible interpretations of the confused words Mac was saying. Then she went over all the possibilities again.

Mac had been injured after leaving her flat. Would he have been thinking about his niece, or about the recent, startling revelations in his own life?

Would he have confused Petra and called her Peter— or was he saying Peterson, and the family, not knowing of her own existence, had assumed he was talking about Petra?

By the time she finished work, Amelia had decided— well, almost decided—on a course of action. She shut herself into a cubicle in the washroom, the only place she knew for sure she'd be undisturbed, and went through it one more time.

In the beginning Mac had left it up to her to decide whether she had the baby or not, but through all the subsequent conversations she'd realised he truly wanted the child she was carrying.

As far as *she* was concerned, the discovery that she was pregnant had been like a miraculous gift, and though she'd been stunned—and concerned about what it would mean in terms of Mac's involvement in her future—there'd been no 'will I, won't I have it' argument in her own mind.

Had she made that clear to Mac?

Did he fear she might not want it?

Was that what was bothering him?

She raised her eyes to the ceiling as she realised for the umpteenth time that if he was worried about the baby— their baby—then she was the only person who could re-assure him.

And the sooner she did it, the better.

Reluctantly, Amelia left her refuge and, after washing her hands and face then swiping a little lipstick on her pale lips, made her way back up to the ICU.

As she got out of the lift her resolve faltered, and shaky knees suggested she retreat.

Think of the baby, she told herself, straightening her shoulders and tilting her chin, as if she were preparing for a battle with officialdom rather than facing a semi-conscious man.

Every child deserved a father.

As luck—good or bad—would have it, the woman she assumed was Mrs McDougal was coming out of the ward.

'Oh,' she said, reaching out and grasping Amelia's arm. 'I've seen you outside the window every day but when I come out to talk to you, you've always disappeared. I'm Marion McDougal, Fraser's mother.'

'I guessed that,' Amelia said, then, realising it was her turn, she held out her hand. 'Amelia Peterson.'

'Peterson! Amelia *Peterson*. Oh, thank heavens. *That's* what he's been saying. We thought he must mean Petra because he's talking about a baby as well, but it didn't make sense. The two of you must be close for him to have been so very anxious about you. Why didn't you come in? Make yourself known? Or did those stupid nurses tell you only family was allowed?'

'I'm actually one of those stupid nurses myself,' Amelia admitted. 'Though downstairs, not up here.'

She stopped, wondering if she was brave enough to take the plunge, then knew she had to see Mac.

'I work with him—we *are* close. I'd like to visit if that's all right with you.'

Marion grasped her hands and pressed them.

'All right? Of course it is. I've just left. I get so upset, seeing him lie there like that, I end up doing more harm than good. And Charlotte, that's his sister, won't be up until her husband gets home to mind the baby. My husband will come back later and sit overnight, but if you could go in now…'

She leant forward and kissed Amelia's cheek.

'Talk to him, tell him things. The neurologist thinks it helps. Seeing you might be just what he needs to get through this stage and up to the next level of recovery.'

Or it might not, Amelia thought as Marion accompanied her back in and told the nursing staff that Amelia should be allowed to visit any time.

Amelia entered the room, aware of the interest of the nurses on duty. It was only because all the other visitors had been family, she told herself, but she knew the grapevine would report differently.

And, like the tendrils on a grapevine, the story would grow.

'You could help by getting yourself out of here, Mac,' she told the still figure on the bed. 'You're not achieving anything just lying there.'

She took his hand and pressed it against her stomach.

'And as you told me once, this is *our* baby I'm carrying. If you think I'm going to bring up the poor little blighter without a father, you've got another think coming.'

The monitor on the wall showed the change in his breathing, then his eyes opened and he looked vacantly around the room for a moment before his gaze fixed on her.

'Peterson? Where the hell have you been?'

His voice was croaky from disuse, but held the usual tone of reprimand—so familiar she felt her heart squeeze with pain.

'Doing your job for you down in A and E,' she told him, holding his fingers tightly and praying she wouldn't cry, at least until she was out of this room.

'And the baby?'

'The baby's fine,' she assured him, then she smiled to herself as his eyelids slid down to cover the usually searching hazel eyes and he drifted back to the nether world he was inhabiting.

She kept hold of his hand and carried on talking, telling him about how work was going, then, thinking it might bother him more than it helped, she talked about her family—about wanting to go into her father's construction business with her brothers until they'd told her she'd be blown off the high-rise building sites.

'They always teased me that they'd taken all the growth genes, which hadn't left much for me.'

Mac stirred and the hand which had lain quiescent in hers moved so his fingers could return her clasp.

'Good genes,' he murmured. 'Glad about that.'

'He's still very confused,' a voice said, and Amelia turned to see a tall, dark-haired, hazel-eyed woman enter the room. 'I'm Charlotte. Do you usually wear jeans that he's talking about them?'

Amelia stood up, knowing the rule about one visitor at a time in the ICU. Then, because it was the easy way out, she agreed with Charlotte that, yes, she usually wore jeans.

Reluctantly, she left the unit, wanting so much to be the one who stayed with Mac. The one to whom he turned when the veil of darkness lifted for a few precious seconds.

'You can go back in the morning,' she reminded herself, then, as an aide turned to look suspiciously at her, she realised she'd spoken aloud.

The man who was in with Mac when Amelia arrived very early the next morning was so much an older version of his son that Amelia felt a beat of familiarity pulse through her veins.

'Ah! So you're Peterson,' he said, leaving the room and joining her outside, extending his hand to Amelia then, instead of shaking it, clasping her fingers in a warm and welcoming grip. 'I'm sure you must have a prettier name than that.'

'Amelia,' she said, looking at the man, wondering why he should be calling her Peterson when his wife and daughter both knew her as Amelia.

'Well, Amelia, I think your visit did the trick,' Mr McDougal told her. 'He's been far more alert during the night. Not all the time. He sleeps a lot, but the doctor says it's an easier sleep, which shows the effect of the concussion is lessening.'

The man hesitated, shifting uneasily and eyeing her cautiously as if waiting for her to say something.

'That's great,' she said, and realised from his expression it wasn't the something he'd been hoping for.

'Yes, it is,' he said, and waited again, but the situation was already confused enough, with Mac's family assuming she and Mac had something going between them.

Well, they did as far as the baby was concerned, but not a relationship...

'I'll leave you, then,' Mr McDougal said, and he walked quietly across to the nurses' station, presumably to check how they felt Mac was doing. But as Amelia walked into the very un-private room, she knew he'd turned to watch her through the glass.

Was he expecting her to greet Mac with a kiss? Watching to see if she did?

She kept her back to the window as she took his hand.

'It's me, Peterson, Mac. I'm back and I'm going to keep coming back and nagging at you until you get yourself out of here.'

'My father knows your father.'

It was such a bizarre thing for him to have said, Amelia decided to ignore it. After all, his eyes were closed and he showed no sign of being conscious, so maybe the statement was part of his confusion.

'Well?'

His eyes opened as he made the demand and he turned his head towards Amelia.

'Aren't you going to say something? Don't you realise what this means? Have you told *your* family yet?'

Amelia slumped down into the chair, still clutching Mac's hand but more to keep a lifeline to sanity than for any other reason.

'Mac, just how conscious are you? Do you know what you're talking about?'

He frowned crossly at her.

'I'm better,' he snapped. 'And I'm talking about our baby and trying to get through into your thick head that as all my family now know about it, and my father apparently sees your father on a fairly regular basis—insurance and golf if I can remember rightly—then the sooner you break the news to your family the better.'

'Well, so much for you doing it with me!' Amelia snapped right back at him, relief at hearing him speaking so rationally touching off post-anxiety anger.

'I can hardly get myself out of here to visit your family,' he grouched. 'And, anyway, it's your fault I'm in here so you'll just have to cope on your own for a bit longer.'

'My fault you're in here? *My* fault?'

'I was thinking about you, Peterson,' he said, 'and then the lights went out. Someone told me a car hit me, but I'm sure I would have been able to dodge it if you hadn't distracted me.'

'Just like a man!' Amelia stood up as she spat the words at him. 'Blame everything on a woman. I really don't know why I bothered to come and see you.'

'Yes, you do,' Mac said softly, and he smiled, dousing Amelia's anger and starting fires of attraction where it had been. 'You want a father for your baby. I distinctly remember you telling me that.'

Then, as if knowing he'd won the point and there was nothing left to say, he closed his eyes and the relaxation of the fingers which had held hers told her he'd drifted back to sleep.

Amelia saw the improvement in Mac each time she stole upstairs for a visit, so she wasn't surprised when Rachel phoned the following morning to tell her he'd been transferred out of the ICU and was now in the neurology ward on the floor below.

'And congratulations, too,' she added. 'Talk about a dark horse—pretending you and Mac were only colleagues. Now I'm hearing about weddings and babies.'

Cold with shock, Amelia blasted Rachel with a few well-chosen words.

'And if I find this story has spread through the hospital, I'll know who to blame,' she finished, trying to sound as threatening as she could.

'What story?' Sally, who was passing the desk at the time, asked. 'The one about you being pregnant with Mac's baby? Boy, did you two keep that relationship quiet!'

Amelia shut her eyes and wondered if it was possible to will oneself to faint. If she could just slide unconscious to the floor, someone would send her home, then she could emigrate to Alaska or perhaps one of the remoter parts of Russia.

She hung up the phone and glared at Sally's back as she disappeared around the corner into the section of A and E where ambulatory patients arrived. Then she tried to think.

It was obvious even to someone with a badly functioning brain and permanently nauseous stomach that if the entire hospital now knew about the baby, it was only a matter of time before her family heard the news. Two of her brothers dated nurses and, though neither worked at St Pat's, gossip spread by osmosis from one hospital to another.

But what did she tell her parents?

That she was pregnant as a result of a really exceptional one-night stand?

No, she'd better leave out the 'really exceptional' part.

'You working today, Peterson, or are you going to sit there dreaming about the biggest grouch in the hospital? Honestly, I can't get my head around it.'

Sally laughed as she added the final sentence, then handed Amelia a list of supplies.

'We're back on track with staff so why don't you do the orders and new rosters and all that paperwork stuff you keep moaning about? After all, as senior nurse, you should be spending more work time at this desk and less with the patients. No other senior works as hard as you.'

Amelia studied the other woman, bemused by Sally's sudden concern for her.

Sally must have read her reaction, for she grinned.

'I'm only suggesting it to save my own skin. Imagine Mac coming back to find you worked to the bone or, worse, to discover you'd lost the baby. He'd kill the lot of us, starting with me because I'm the 2IC.'

'But you can't mollycoddle me right through the pregnancy,' Amelia said, the shock she was feeling making her voice sound faint and the words feeble.

'Of course not,' Sally declared. 'Just till Mac gets back, then I'm quite sure he'll take over.'

She left the list on the desk and walked away. Amelia pulled the piece of paper towards her but her eyes wouldn't focus on it when her mind was following through on Sally's comment.

Mac taking over?

It was a sobering thought—no, it was a frightening thought. Mac was a born autocrat—delivering orders like gunshots. If she let him think for one moment he could run her life as he ran A and E...

The images flashing through her mind reinforced her decision to avoid marrying Mac at all costs.

Though with his family and all the staff now assuming marriage...

Mac's family is not your problem at the moment, she reminded herself, and turned her attention, not to the list but to how to tell her parents she was pregnant.

Gulp!

Aware of the urgency of the situation, she lifted the phone and called her mother. No reply, though the answering machine eventually came on.

'Mum, it's me, Amelia. I thought I'd come over for dinner tonight. If that doesn't suit, could you phone me at work.'

Double gulp—but it was done. Now she could concentrate on work. This time she did focus on the list, and then the roster, and after that she finalised the work she'd been doing on the staff training programme and emailed her suggestions off to the DON.

'Actually going to do some real work, are you?' Brian teased, as she came out of the cubby-hole behind the admissions desk.

'I thought I might,' she told him. 'And I'm starting with an inspection of all treatment rooms and cubicles. You've been on restocking this week, haven't you?'

Brian groaned. 'Come on, Peterson. You know what

this place has been like lately. You can't expect perfect restocking. Besides, the night shift are supposed to do it.'

'Every shift is supposed to do it,' she reminded him. 'A and E on the evening shift can be a war zone—it's our duty as day shift staff to make sure everything's on hand for the evening staff, and you know it. The place is still quiet, so I'll give you an hour before I inspect.'

He walked away, muttering under his breath, no doubt about pregnant women being touchy, but she took no notice. She'd grouched herself about restocking from time to time. It was not only an uninteresting job, but a tedious one as well because of the forms that needed to be completed for every request. But if they had, as did happen from time to time, a patient who'd taken half his arm off in an industrial or farm accident, and there were not enough pressure pads on an emergency trolley, precious minutes could be lost.

She went back into the cubby-hole and made a note to remind herself to talk about the seemingly unimportant jobs that were part of A and E work at the next staff meeting.

The phone rang as she was leaving.

'Sister Peterson? This is Tony Wheeler, Charge Nurse in Neurology. Could you come up?'

'Is it Mac? Has something happened?'

'You could say that,' the nurse said in a tone dry enough to shrivel skin.

Amelia dropped the phone and rushed out, through to the lift foyer where, fortunately for her sanity, a lift was going up.

'What's happened? Where is he?' she demanded of the only male at the nurses' station.

'Room six one six,' the man replied, nodding his head in the direction of the far end of the ward.

Amelia kept going, arriving at the single room in time to hear Mac's roar.

'I'm a doctor and I know how I am. Do you think anyone can get better lying around in a madhouse like this? And stop arguing, Mum, because there is no way I'm going home to your unit. I'm thirty-five. Thirty-five-year-olds don't go home to Mother.'

Amelia pushed through the door and all but ran into the backs of a nurse and Mrs McDougal who, considering the rage emanating from Mac, had bravely positioned themselves in front of the door, apparently to prevent his escape.

'You're obviously better,' she said over their shoulders to Mac. 'Right back to your rude, cantankerous self. But if I were you, I'd sit down. Your "well enough to go home" argument won't be nearly as effective if you're lying flat out on the floor in a dead faint.'

Mac frowned at her, but he did sit down. On the bed, not a chair, so he still looked taller and more authoritative than anyone else in the room.

'Good. Now, what's this commotion all about?'

Mac's 'I want to go home' was echoed by two versions of 'He wants to go home' uttered in identical tones of disbelief.

'Mac, you've just been transferred down from the ICU—you should at least spend one night here under observation.'

Mac glowered at her.

'Under observation! Do you know what that means, Peterson? No, of course you don't. But I've been here four hours and I do know. It means every time you drift off to sleep, some fussy, bossy, know-it-all nurse comes in and wakes you up to take your temperature or blood pressure or ask you how you're feeling. I can understand why half the poor sods down in and A and E practically cry when we tell them we have to admit them. Some even die rather than face the same fate.'

Amelia listened to the delivery of his speech more than the words. After all, the words were typical Mac-letting-off-steam words, but they weren't slurred and he definitely didn't sound confused.

She studied the way he sat, arms folded and eyes half-closed—brooding but determined. Fraser McDougal had no intention of remaining in hospital.

'Well, he's probably just as well off at home as he is here,' Amelia told the two women, 'as long as there's someone around who can keep an eye on him.'

She considered the 'him' in question and shook her head, while the nurse, with a quiet 'He's all yours', disappeared out the door.

'Stupid thing to say.' Amelia corrected herself. 'As if he'd listen to advice on looking after himself from any-one—but it would be good if there was someone around to phone an ambulance if he collapsed.'

Ignoring the growling noise Mac was making, Amelia turned to his mother.

'Does he have neighbours who'd look in?'

Mrs McDougal began to speak, then stopped, a flush of what could only be embarrassment creeping into her cheeks.

'Of course not,' Amelia guessed. 'He's probably been rude to all of them.'

'I have not!' Mac snapped. 'Mrs Warren thinks I'm wonderful.'

'Mrs Warren is about two hundred years old and deaf,' Marion said, 'and he fell out with the neighbour on the other side. And then there are the stairs—the bedroom and bathroom are upstairs, the kitchen and living room downstairs. Dr Blake said he could suffer dizziness.'

She looked helplessly at Amelia, and while Mac was explaining that the neighbour on the other side was a certified lunatic and a witch to boot, Marion McDougal said haltingly to Amelia, 'Do you—would you—could you?'

Sleep over sometimes?

Look after him?

Perhaps have him at your place?

Amelia's quick mind obligingly finished the halting half-sentences. Of course the woman would assume they slept together—how else could she, Amelia, be pregnant?

And the thought of Mac falling down the stairs of his townhouse was truly horrifying.

'You'd better come to my place. I've got three days off, and can probably take some holiday time after that if necessary. But that's on condition you stay here overnight. You need at least twenty-four hours of monitoring before you go home.'

She gave him a stern look.

'So get back into bed and stop hassling the nursing staff when they're only doing their duty. I'll speak to Doug Blake about cutting back the obs to two-hourly, and in return you try being co-operative.'

Mac looked slightly stunned by her performance, but he did swing his legs back up onto the bed and lean back against the pillows, though the way his arms were folded suggested he was simply marshalling his next argument.

Marion, on the other hand, was obviously delighted with this outcome. She beamed at Amelia and gave her a hug.

'You have no idea what a relief that is to me,' she said, then she gave Amelia another hug. 'Or how happy I am about your other news. I know you probably didn't mean for it to come out like this, but I know how much Fraser has always longed for a child.'

Amelia accepted the hug, but over Marion McDougal's shoulder she caught a glimpse of Mac's face. He was frowning again—but not his usual fierce 'frighten all the juniors' frown, more a worried kind of frown.

She untangled herself from the grateful arms and walked across to where Mac still sat on the bed.

'It'll be OK,' she said very quietly, offering him the assurances he'd offered her about the pregnancy. 'We'll work it out.'

His eyes sought hers, questioning and wary.

Mac wary?

'The thing is, Peterson—' he began in a husky whisper, just as she decided his expression was more worried than wary.

Amelia lifted her hand and pressed a finger to his lips.

'Shh. Not now. We'll talk later.'

Which should have ended the matter, but Mac's lips opened and the tip of his tongue caressed her finger, sending shocks like lightning bolts through Amelia's body.

She was fighting the effect of these when he moved, sitting up and swinging his legs back to the floor. Then he reached out and pulled her closer, parting his legs so she ended up between his thighs.

'Mum's tactfully withdrawn so if we're not talking until later, maybe we can find something better to do with our lips.'

He cupped one hand behind her head, then leaned forward so his lips met hers—sweetly, cleanly, masterfully.

His hand slipped from her head to her back, pressing her up against his torso, and when, realising this wasn't exactly prescribed behaviour between a nurse and a patient, Amelia tried to back away, he lifted his head long enough to murmur, 'You know you shouldn't argue with head-injured patients, or aggravate them in any way.' Then he continued to kiss her with a hunger that fired far too much need in her own body.

Eventually, Amelia escaped, but not before she'd given way to her own feelings and returned the kiss with unfamiliar delight.

'I'll see you later,' she said, as she straightened her uniform and hoped she didn't look as confused as she felt.

Mac nodded, but the worried look was back on his face, so now Amelia had to worry about what Mac might be worrying about, as well as her own confusion.

But how could she guess what Mac was worrying about?

Dismissing Mac's worries, she focussed on her own.

Was her jolting reaction to the kiss another sign she might actually be in love with Mac?

Boy, was that a humungously frightening concept! How could anyone possibly be in love with Mac?

And how would he handle it if she was?

Forget him—how would *she* handle it?

As best she could—that's how.

As long as she didn't have to live with him…

She returned to A and E where the slow pace of the morning had been replaced by something resembling Friday night chaos.

'Gas leak in the city. I was about to page you. Mostly breathing difficulties, no serious casualties so far, but the ambulances brought this lot in anyway.'

Sally waved her hand towards a scattering of people, sitting in the waiting room with oxygen masks held to their faces.

'One asthmatic in cubicle three. Brian's in there but he's due on lunch, so if you want to take over?'

Amelia took over, checked the patient and the file, then, as the young woman seemed comfortable, she glanced around, pleased to see the glove dispensers on the wall were positively bursting with gloves and the trolley was carefully and fully stocked.

'Do I have to stay here?' the young woman asked, and Amelia, thinking of Mac and his very different demands to escape the hospital environs, explained that she'd be released as soon as a doctor had been back to check on her.

'As far as I can see, there's no reason to keep you,' she told the patient.

Rick Stewart appeared as she spoke, and Amelia smiled to herself as the patient quickly removed the oxygen mask and patted down her hair. Rick was tall and blond with killer blue eyes and was considered one of the best-looking doctors on staff. Though, Amelia found herself thinking, she preferred a dark, craggy kind of good looks.

Since when?

Since you kissed him less than an hour ago?

Similar arguments wrangled in her head throughout the rest of the day, so by four, when she signed off from one responsibility and went up to visit another, she was mentally exhausted.

And physically?

Confused, excited, apprehensive, jittery—a very dicey cocktail of emotions swirled in her body.

But she was a professional—a nurse with a patient to tend. All she had to do was think of Mac that way and the rest should be easy.

'Like skinning an elephant would be easy,' she muttered to herself.

Doug Blake caught her as she exited the lift, and guilt

swamped her. She'd had no time to contact him about the obs.

'I've just seen Mac and cut back his obs to two-hourly—it was that or be responsible for him causing bodily harm to a poor unfortunate nurse. I hear you're taking him home in the morning.' He rolled his eyes in mock disbelief and added, 'You *do* realise what you're tackling?'

Amelia straightened up and looked the specialist right in the eye. 'Mac might be a bit of a tyrant at work, but it's how he gets things done, and underneath that gruff—'

'And grouchy!' Doug interjected.

'And grouchy—' Amelia accepted the word with gritted teeth '—exterior, there's a kind and caring individual.'

'Very individual!' Doug said, but he smiled at her, and his gaze flipped down her figure. 'I guess you've seen his finer points.'

Amelia felt her cheeks burn but she refused to back down.

'Have you any orders you want followed—any *medical* advice to give me before I take him home?'

Doug stopped smiling, and shrugged as if he accepted that whatever advice he gave would be useless.

'Try to keep him quiet. He shouldn't read for long and definitely shouldn't watch television for a week or two. Ideally, he should have stayed in hospital a couple more days, but he won't and you're the next best thing.'

He put out his hand.

'Good luck!'

Amelia shook it, but she didn't return the smile he offered. She was damned if she was going to smile at a man who made Mac sound like a monster.

He was lying on the bed with his eyes closed, so still Amelia assumed he was asleep. She stopped just inside the door and looked at him, her heart tripping in its beat as she thought of what might have happened.

But the trip in her heartbeat was nothing to the rapid acceleration that followed when she realised just what she was taking on. Not only would she have the responsibility of taking care of Mac while he recuperated, but she'd have him in her home, twenty-four hours a day, and she'd have the attraction she'd been at such odds to deny hammering at her for sixty seconds of every minute and sixty minutes of every one of those twenty-four hours.

I must be mad! she thought, then wondered if she was talking to herself again when Mac opened his eyes.

'You can come right in. I don't bite.'

That made Amelia smile.

'No?' she said. 'Tell that to the troops downstairs. Or the nurses on this floor.'

Mac sat up, slowly enough to tell Amelia he was still far from well.

'Are you sure you should be going home?' Anxiety for him prompted the question which she regretted the moment she saw the frown gather on his brow.

'I'm not exactly going home, am I?' he growled. 'And it's not until tomorrow anyway.'

Amelia bit back an urge to tell him that she didn't want him at her place any more than he wanted to be there. In fact, she'd have liked to have told him exactly where he *could* go, but she reminded herself he was a patient first and Mac second, and after all she'd offered to have him.

He reached under the bed and pulled out a duffel bag, then fiddled in one of its pockets, finally producing a key. The frown was back as he flipped it lightly up and down in his hand, then looked at her.

'Know anything about retrograde amnesia?'

Apart from 'Will you marry me?', it was the last question Amelia had expected.

'Retrograde amnesia?'

Repeating the question didn't help, and before she could think what to say, Mac was speaking again.

'Not a lot—I thought not. I wondered if you'd mind going out to my place for a couple of medical books and some clothes. Mum brought in pyjamas but there's no way I'm walking out of here in them, and I'll need a couple of clean shirts and underdaks for the time I'm with you.'

He gave her another doubtful look and added, 'Unless I have enough at your place.'

It didn't take much to put retrograde amnesia and the remark about clothes together. Great jumping giants! He'd come out of the accident and remembered about her being pregnant, then must have assumed they'd had an ongoing relationship of some kind which he *couldn't* remember.

'Retrograde amnesia is a gap in memory of events in a particular part of the past,' she told him. 'Usually just before the accident. But you remembered about the baby, and leaving my place to drive home, so it's unlikely you've got memory loss. Anyway, Doug Blake said you weren't allowed to read so I'll get the clothes but forget the books.'

She reached out to take the key, but his fingers trapped hers, closing around her hand and holding it tightly.

'What about anterograde amnesia—forgetting specific events or a specific time in the past?'

Uncertainty leant the question an edge of desperation, and the fact that this was Mac being uncertain affected Amelia more than she could fully understand.

She leaned closer and put her free arm around his shoulders, drawing his head towards her body and giving him a tight, comforting hug.

'There's nothing wrong with your memory,' she assured him, and was about to explain when he released her hand and pulled her even closer, his lips finding her breast before teasing their way up her throat, along her jaw-line and finally, while Amelia still fought for control of the sensations he was causing, captured her lips.

CHAPTER EIGHT

MAC'S surge of desire defeated his aching head, and his arms tightened around Peterson's slight frame. His lips drank in her sweetness, while his body burned with a fierce pride that soon the slim, pliant figure would swell with the growth of his child.

Their child!

OK, so he might be a little hazy over the details of their relationship, like how long it had been going on and where it was conducted—it had to have been at her place as he certainly had no recollection of her ever having been at his—but he'd definitely made the right choice this time as far as a marriage partner was concerned.

The thought of being married to Peterson was so intoxicating his kiss deepened, becoming more demanding, so it wasn't until she pushed away, muttering somewhat breathlessly 'This is not the time or place for this, Mac', that he remembered where they were.

'I could come home with you right now,' he suggested.

Her brown eyes scanned his face, and he read worry in their dark depths. He stroked his fingers along her chin and up to her temple where a vein throbbed beneath the fine skin.

'Don't look so worried, Little Bug,' he said, the nickname coming so easily off his lips he realised he'd often thought of her that way. 'I said I'd stay overnight in this wretched hospital and I will.'

He smoothed the satiny skin.

'I don't ever want you worrying over me—so if I ever

134

do anything to upset you in any way, you just tell me, OK?'

Amusement banished most of the worry in her eyes, and her lips tilted into a tantalising smile.

'And you'll immediately desist?' she teased. 'Now, why do I find that hard to imagine?'

The teasing prompted him to kiss her again, but though she responded with a passion that left him both breathless and aching with desire, he remembered that remnant of worry and after she'd departed, muttering about dinner at her parents' and already being late, he couldn't help thinking about it.

Amelia left the neurology ward but, late though she was, she didn't go straight to her parents' place. Instead, she went back down to A and E where she phoned home to say she was running late, then found a phone book to look up Mac's address—praying he wasn't paranoid enough about privacy to have an unlisted number.

Relief surged through her as she not only found the address she needed but realised it was in a suburb not far from her family home. But the relief was short-lived when she remembered just why she was going home.

There was no easy way to do it, she finally decided, pulling up outside the house where she'd grown up. She'd just have to march straight in there and tell them.

Easier said than done, she realised as her mother greeted her with a kiss and a hug, then scolded her for not getting home more often, being too thin, not looking after herself properly then demanding to know if she was getting enough sleep.

'I'm fine, Mum,' Amelia said, moving out of the embrace and looking into her mother's so-familiar face. 'But I've got something to tell you.'

'Whatever it is, darling, it can't be bad enough to make you frown like that.'

Amelia smiled at her mother's assurance.

'Or bad enough to drum me from the family?' she joked, then remembered her excitement about the baby. 'It's actually not bad, just unexpected.'

And was that an understatement when you considered the how and who of this situation!

'I'm pregnant, Mum.'

Her mother's reaction was sheer delight. She opened up her arms and drew her daughter close.

'Oh, darling, that's so wonderful!' Then she pushed Amelia away and looked at her again. 'It *is* wonderful, isn't it? You're happy about it? You want this baby?'

Amelia relished the warm-hearted acceptance then felt tears prick behind her eyelids.

'Oh, Mum, I want it so much. All those years with Brad, when it didn't happen, now it's like a miracle.'

Her mother hugged her again, then said, 'Come on, we'll tell your father. The boys all seem to be enjoying bachelorhood too much to marry and settle down, so Dad and I were beginning to think we'd never have a grand-child.'

She hasn't asked about the father, Amelia realised as she followed in her mother's wake. Too tactful?

Her father, though, went straight to the point.

'And the father? Is he going to be involved? Is he happy about the baby or will he opt out and leave you to bring up the child on your own?'

'We'll help and always be there for you,' her mother said quickly, as if to soften her husband's words. 'Your father can settle a trust fund on it, so you won't have financial worries.'

Amelia smiled, warmed by her mother's quick assurances of support.

But it was her father who wanted an answer.

'Actually, he's very happy about it,' she said, ignoring the mental reminder that this hadn't been unequivocally confirmed by the man in question. 'It's Mac, Fraser McDougal. I've spoken of him to you. He's the doctor in charge of A and E.'

'The ogre? The one who yells at you?' Her mother's disbelief was palpable.

'He only yells at work,' Amelia told her, though she knew this would probably prove untrue and Mac would yell just as much at home if she dared to disobey his directives, particularly in regard to the health and welfare of his unborn child.

'Fraser McDougal.' Her father repeated Mac's name as if running a mental scan of his memory. 'Wasn't he in an accident just recently? I noticed it in the paper. Only picked up the name because I know his father. A fine man, Alec McDougal, and very proud of his son, the doctor. You've met him, too, Meg. Allied Insurance.'

'He was in an accident? Is he all right?' her mother demanded, ignoring the rest of her husband's explanation.

Amelia remembered the passionate kiss she and Mac had shared, and grinned.

'He needs rest more than anything. He's still in hospital but I'm taking him home to my place tomorrow.'

Both parents nodded as if this was a perfectly natural thing to be doing, then her mother ushered them both into the kitchen, where Amelia's sense of homecoming was always strongest. It was a huge room, dominated by the table in the middle where the family had always gathered for all but the most formal of meals. Here she'd talked and joked with her brothers, discussed everything from puberty to gun laws with her parents and siblings and learned to cherish the warmth and values of family life.

To Amelia's relief, though they talked a lot about the baby, neither of her parents raised the dicey issue of marriage.

Though as she drove away, heading for Mac's place, she knew for certain that what she wanted for this child was a family life like she had known herself—with the warmth and security of two loving parents, preferably united in marriage.

Which would mean marrying Mac.

Even if he doesn't love you?

The excitement that had risen at the thought of marriage to the man she suspected she loved plummeted again, and unlocking the door to his townhouse caused even more apprehension. It wasn't as if she was breaking in, so why should she feel this way?

Because it was Mac's place, and entering it suggested an intimacy that didn't exist between them.

Ignoring the yammer of apprehension in her head, she felt for a light-switch, then stared in dismay at the bare, soulless living room the light revealed. A big leather armchair, a television set and bookcases jam-packed, untidily, with books and magazines.

A dining table and four chairs stood at the far end of the room, with more medical and scientific magazines stacked on its surface. No pictures adorned the walls, no cushions softened the hard wooden chairs, no patterned tablecloth or plant or flowers decorated the table. Amelia thought of her brothers' apartments—two of them in her apartment complex—and though they were all obviously bachelor dens, they exuded an atmosphere that suggested they'd made them homes.

Uncertain now about why this place should seem so

bleak, she walked through the narrow room towards the kitchen. Here, the benches were so clean Amelia suspected his mother had cleaned up when she'd come to collect Mac's pyjamas. But the cleanliness reinforced the bleakness of the place.

Upstairs, a small bedroom at the front had been converted to an office—more magazines, books and papers—while the larger bedroom behind it was as soulless as his living room, with a bed and a dressing-table with no clutter marring its surface, though a framed photo lay face down on its surface. And a bedside table—only one—as if no one ever shared the bed.

Unable to resist, she crossed to the dressing-table and lifted the photo, setting it upright then studying the image. A serenely beautiful woman looked back at her. Though it was a black and white portrait, Amelia could tell the woman's hair was blonde, and her eyes were undoubtedly blue.

Huh! Blue-eyed blonde—what a cliché! Unexpected jealousy soured Amelia's stomach, but she couldn't halt her thoughts. Considering Helene, maybe blondes were Mac's preference.

But who was this woman, and why hadn't she put in an appearance at the hospital?

And why hadn't Mac taken *her* to dinner with him that fateful night at Capriccio's?

Involuntarily, a memory of the crumpled receipt from Capriccio's returned to Amelia, but she thrust it aside, opening the built-in cupboards and searching through them for what might be considered appropriate 'convalescing' clothes. She selected four shirts, a couple of sweaters, two pairs of jeans and an assortment of underwear. Wishing she'd thought of borrowing a bag from home, she balanced the load in her arms and, after turning off the upstairs lights, started down the stairs.

The clothes were clean, yet held a distinctly masculine odour, so it was almost as if she was holding Mac in her arms again.

'Oh, dear!' she murmured, pushing her face against one of the sweaters and breathing in the scent of him. 'Surely it can't be love.'

Mentally reassuring herself that, of course, she couldn't be in love with Mac, she walked through to the kitchen to check there was nothing going green in his refrigerator.

No, all clear—his mother must have checked in here as well.

Or perhaps the blonde...

Nonsense! Amelia told herself. Don't start obsessing about someone you don't even know.

She stood perfectly still, squeezing her eyes tightly shut, concentrating on banishing the hot stabs of doubt and jealousy from her brain. Then she thrust her face into his clothes again, and reminded herself he was hers for at least the next three days.

A tap on the window startled her, and she looked up to see the photo turned to flesh. The cliché was smiling and waving at her, and on legs so heavy with reluctance she could barely make them move, Amelia walked towards the back door and opened it.

'I'm Jessica—Mac's neighbour.' The woman managed to make the last word sound so suggestive Amelia flinched.

A neighbour? Well, this one certainly wasn't two hundred and Amelia doubted she was deaf...

Jessica was looking her up and down. 'Ah, you're a nurse. I see you're taking clothes up to him. Does that mean he's coming home?'

'Not for a few days,' Amelia said, feeling perkier now as she remembered Mac's description of this woman as a witch. He hadn't sounded as if he was madly in love with her.

Though maybe she'd left him for someone else, and his scorn was camouflage for jealousy and heartache.

'Well, give him my love, won't you?' Jessica flashed a dazzling smile at Amelia. 'The poor darling knows I can't handle hospitals so he'll understand why I haven't been to visit, but I'll be here for him when he does come home—tell him that as well.'

She flipped her fingers in another little wave, and disappeared back out the door.

'I'd rather cut my tongue out,' Amelia muttered savagely to herself, locking the door securely, then marching through the living room and out the front door.

Once in the car, anger suggested she drive straight to the hospital and ask Mac exactly where this Jessica stood in his life, but he'd probably be sleeping. And even with the obs cut back to two-hourly, he was being woken often enough, so waking him again wasn't a good idea.

She drove home and carried his clothes up from the car park. Once inside her apartment, another dilemma presented itself. Which bedroom?

He's an invalid and needs rest, she reminded herself, but she knew, from the heated kisses they'd been sharing, that rest would be the last thing on Mac's mind when he arrived here in the morning.

She put the clothes into the spare bedroom anyway, telling herself there was no room in her cupboards and that he might like his privacy.

Then she went to bed and lay there, staring at the ceiling, unable to believe the tides of fate that had brought her to this point.

And unable to imagine where they'd wash her next.

Into bed with Mac, that's where, Amelia realised a little over twelve hours later. Ignoring all her protestations that he was supposed to rest and definitely not get excited, he'd swept her into his arms within seconds of their arrival at her apartment, and from there the path had led inevitably to bed.

He was sleeping now, his body sprawled beside her, a suggestion of a smile on his beautifully sculpted lips.

'Oh, Mac,' she murmured, her eyes cataloguing the familiar features as if she needed to imprint them in her brain.

For a time when he'd no longer be lying in her bed?

She couldn't answer because she didn't know, but uneasiness lurked beneath the pleasant and well-satisfied weariness she was feeling. Her attachment to Mac was starting to feel a whole lot like love, but wasn't she deceiving him, letting him think their affair had been an ongoing thing, not just a boozy, though thoroughly wonderful, one-night stand?

And then there was Jessica…

Shifting uneasily—conscience prodding, perhaps—she was about to slide out of the bed when he rolled over, and with a lazy arm drew her close, tucking her so comfortably up against his body she decided she'd accept the sheer magic of snuggling close to Mac and worry about deception later.

Mac woke to a bundle of softness in his arms, and smiled as he remembered, tucking the sleeping Peterson even closer to his body. Right now he was thinking maybe it hadn't been such a good idea as the soft body in his arms stirred more than memory. He *was* convalescent and, though Doug had put no specific limits on sexual endeavours, he had explained in far too graphic detail why Mac needed to rest in order for his battered brain to heal completely.

Would he then remember more about his and Peterson's relationship?

He had no idea!

Did it matter if he didn't?

He thought this one through and decided it didn't—not particularly as far as he was concerned. As long as Peterson— Had he stopped calling her that before the accident? Had he been murmuring 'Amelia' into her ear? Well, as long as she didn't know he couldn't remember, it would be OK.

Damn it all—he could recall that first momentous night so clearly, as if the unexpected magic of it was stamped in his mind, while his body only had to think of their love-making on that occasion to become excited about repeating the performance.

So he'd better not think about it now—just about the baby, and Peterson, and how fate had finally singled him out for a bit of good luck for a change.

She murmured in her sleep and he brushed a long strand of hair from her eyes, smoothing it back then twining his fingers in the softness. He could definitely remember doing that before—remember how it had brushed across his chest when she'd leaned over him to kiss him. How it had made a dark curtain around their faces, adding a touch of mystery to their journey of discovery.

Actually, he'd better get out of bed, because the combination of the memories he *had* retained, and Peterson's closeness, were prompting ideas that weren't even close to rest.

*   *   *

Amelia woke refreshed but anxious—she was alone in the bed.

Fine nurse you are, she chided herself. Home for a couple of hours and you've lost your patient.

He was in the living room, stretched out in one of her leather recliners, sleeping soundly. And seeing him there, she decided she'd forget about the deception. She'd make the most of the present—take care of him while he convalesced, enjoy having him in her apartment and see what happened after that.

When he remembers you've not been having an affair?

Amelia shook away the thought, physically twitching against the prickles of conscience, and went into the kitchen to check on what she could offer in the way of lunch. Some time today, she'd have to shop.

The mundane domestic considerations soothed her agitation, and she went quietly back into her room, where she showered and, with the rest of the day free—apart from shopping—took the opportunity to wash her hair. She was in her bedroom, blow-drying it, when Mac came in.

'I'm sorry if the dryer woke you—it's a noisy thing.'

'I was ready to wake up,' he said, taking the dryer and the brush from her unresisting fingers, then settling himself behind her on the bed and taking over the task.

Her arms, which always ached halfway through the process, were grateful, but the rest of her body told her it was not a good idea. Sitting so close to Mac, with his fingers lifting and brushing her hair, sent vibrant transmissions of desire scooting along her nerves.

His, too, she guessed when he used a handful of hair to gently tug her closer.

'You have to rest,' she reminded him.

'Later,' he whispered, but he continued with the task in hand, although every time he now touched her hair, it was a caress—a prelude to the loving that would follow as certainly as sunrise heralded the day.

CHAPTER NINE

THREE days with Mac, talking to him, sleeping with him—laughing, scolding, teasing—was like a lifetime, yet all too soon this brief interlude had passed, and Amelia had to return to work.

'I should be going back as well,' Mac told her, holding her in his arms inside her front door as if he never wanted to let her go. 'I can't just sit around here, doing nothing.'

'You can rest,' Amelia whispered, pressing little kisses on his lips. 'It's what you're supposed to have been doing all along.'

'But I'm well enough to go back to work,' he protested, between nibbling at her ear and nuzzling his lips down her neck to a sensitive spot he'd discovered earlier.

'You're not, and you know it.' She moved slightly away and touched her fingers to his temple. 'You're still suffering headaches and I'm going to talk to Doug Blake about them today. You should have another scan.'

'Speaking of which,' he said, pressing his hand, as he often did, against her abdomen, 'when do we see the first pictures of Junior?'

'Oh, heavens! Not for ages, surely,' Amelia replied, realising, with a jolt, that she'd forgotten about the baby.

'You should see an O and G man. Charlotte went to Peter Chan.'

'There's plenty of time.' Amelia pressed a final kiss on Mac's lips. 'Right now we have to get you better, and I've got to go to work. You can read for half an hour at a time but no television.'

'Bossy!' he chided, but he returned her kiss, holding her close for a minute until she pulled away, knowing she'd be late if they took the clinch any further.

She drove to work, her mind whirling. Apart from a few quick dashes to the shops, it was the first time she'd been away from Mac for the three days—the first time she had a chance to think.

So what had changed?

She felt herself blush—her sex life for a start.

Forget the sex! Get real here.

The *real* problem in Amelia's life right now was how she felt about Mac. She no longer had to ask herself if she was in love with him. The knowledge sang in her veins and thudded in her heart whenever she looked at him, or heard his voice, or even, like now, thought about him.

And it changed the 'going it alone' scenario somewhat, because now she had to consider if being with him all the time, albeit in a loveless marriage, might not be better than not being with him...

She swung her car into the entrance to the staff car park and sighed. As far as she could make out, Mac had given no consideration to the love thing. He was certainly loving, and when he called her 'Little Bug', and sometimes even a huskily whispered 'Amelia', her foolish heart skipped with pleasure, grasping these as endearments. But, rationally, she knew they were words linked to their passion, and passion was soon spent.

Then there was his loving, eager neighbour...

Amelia glared at the driver who pulled into the vacant car space she'd noticed, then sighed again. There were too many cars and not enough spaces—too many questions and not enough answers.

And on top of that, she realised, finally finding a parking space in the far corner of the lot, she now had to walk into A and E and cope with all the questions she knew would be flung at her.

She'd answer any about Mac's state of health—improving every day, she'd say—but that was it. Anything else anyone asked, she'd just ignore.

She got through the day by working flat out, making some changes suggested by the DON to her programme for the in-service training, supervising the young student Allison Wright through her first trauma patient, tending patients herself and chivvying her staff into more efficient responses.

'I hope you don't intend to keep up this pace right through your pregnancy,' Sally said to her, as they both collapsed into chairs in the tearoom at the end of their shift. 'I can handle obsessive-compulsive behaviour occasionally, but for an entire pregnancy?'

'It was not obsessive-compulsive behaviour,' Amelia said with great dignity. 'Just putting things right. I take three days off and the place falls apart.'

'Tell that to the marines!' Sally scoffed. 'My guess is you're missing Mac, and working hard makes the time go faster, so before you know it you'll be back in his loving arms.'

She hooted with laughter at the thought of anyone wanting to get back to Mac's arms, but Amelia acknowledged Sally was partly right. She'd worked flat out so she'd had no time to think of anything but the job. When she was with Mac, all her doubts and fears were set aside, her mind and body consumed by the delight of being with him. But when he wasn't there, the black thoughts flooded in.

Along with images of Jessica...

*   *   *

There was only one way to tackle the Jessica matter, she decided, arriving home to find her house guest once again asleep on her reclining chair.

She'd ask.

'Bug? You're home? How was it? How are things at work? Who's doing my job? Tell me it's not Rick Stewart—that bastard's had his eyes set on my position since he first started practising medicine. I know he thinks I've forgotten, but I remember him as an intern. Flashy looks the girls all fall for, and no substance.'

Amelia forgot about Jessica and laughed.

'Oh, Mac, you should hear yourself! As if the hospital would ever replace you—especially now when, Colleen was telling me, there's a chance St Pat's will get the nod as Lakelands' major trauma centre.'

She walked past him to the kitchen to put down some groceries she'd bought on her way home, then turned to find him right behind her.

'I've missed you,' he muttered, while the crooked smile accompanying the words suggested he might actually have meant them.

He reached out and drew her close, just holding her as if to reassure himself she *had* returned.

And Amelia, taking comfort from this simple hug, nestled closer.

'If I start to kiss you we'll never eat,' he whispered, pulling pins out of her hair and combing it down her back with his fingers. 'And as I've got dinner almost cooked, and I'm not skilled enough to keep things warm, why don't you have a shower, slip into something comfortable, then come back and have a drink before I serve up?'

Amelia looked up into his face and frowned.

'You've cooked dinner?'

'I *can* cook!' The defensive retort was more like the Mac she knew, and she smiled.

'I've never doubted it for a moment, but—'

He silenced her with the kiss he'd said they shouldn't have, then broke off before it became too heated.

'Go shower, woman!' he ordered, turning her and giving her a little push in the direction of the bathroom.

Amelia went, but she was worrying again. Isn't it getting all a bit too domestic? was what she'd been going to say. Had Mac guessed this, that he'd silenced her?

Was he already thinking of returning to his own soulless townhouse?

To his sexy blonde neighbour?

Was he having second thoughts about the future he'd mentioned earlier—about marriage?

And if so, what would happen when his convalescence was over?

CHAPTER TEN

NOTHING! That's what happened when Mac's convalescence was over. Not only did he show no sign of moving out, but gradually more and more of his clothes materialised in Amelia's apartment.

'You didn't drive over to your place, did you?' she demanded, when she returned from a late shift to find a bundle of suits slung over the back of her lounge.

As well as being car-less, his having been written off in the accident, driving was still on the list of things he couldn't do. She drove him to work when she was working the early shift, and he took a cab when she was, like today, working late.

'No, Carl picked me up from the hospital and drove me over to the townhouse. I tell you, Bug, you've got the most obliging set of brothers, but I can't help feeling they're being so helpful so they can keep an eye on how I'm treating you. And they're all such big lads, too. I hope they never think I'm doing the wrong thing.'

He lifted the pile of clothes and walked away, taking them through to the second bedroom where she'd first put his clothes.

She watched his broad back disappear down the passageway and wondered if, somewhere among the clothes, he'd tucked the picture of Jessica. Amelia was considering the ethics of a bit of snooping—and coming down against such low behaviour—when he returned.

'He thought it was a bit odd we were still maintaining two homes.'

Amelia, tired after a long shift, eyed her lover warily. She knew him well enough by now to know he didn't say things simply to break the silence or hear his own voice. Most of Mac's conversations led somewhere.

But even as she was considering this, another bit of her brain was thinking about the 'Carl drove me over' statement, and realising just how far he'd inveigled himself into her life. Once news of her pregnancy had whipped through the family, Carl and Rob, the two brothers who lived in this same building, had appeared, apparently to offer congratulations, but Amelia knew it had been to check out the man who'd suddenly entered their sister's life.

Far from being any threat to Mac, their approval had been obvious, and often Amelia had returned from work to find one or other, and sometimes even Alistair, who hated city living and had a house in an outer suburb, playing war-based board games with Mac around her dining table.

'I suppose it's only because Rowley's touring that he's not half living here as well,' she muttered grouchily, then, as Mac frowned, she realised how far her mind had strayed. 'What were we talking about?'

He walked around the lounge and dropped down to sit beside her, putting his arm along the back of it so she could feel its closeness even though he wasn't touching her.

Mac lifted his hand and automatically began to take the pins from the thick bunch of shiny dark hair, already imagining how it would look and feel as it tumbled from captivity. Would his fascination with it ever wane?

Would his attraction to Peterson ever grow less?

He rather hoped so—just marginally perhaps—as surely

he'd be old and burnt out before his time if his sex life kept going the way it was.

He clamped down on thoughts of sex and, knowing it was important, tried to remember what they'd been talking about. But Peterson looked tired, and he trailed the back of his fingers down her cheek.

'Would you miss work very much if you gave it up?' he asked. 'Or cut back?'

She turned and frowned at him.

'Now, where did that come from?' she demanded. 'I might not remember what you did ask, but it certainly wasn't about work.'

He used his hand to tug her closer, then massaged her neck and shoulders.

'You look tired. I've not only got you pregnant but I've been an added burden to you, being here, needing to be looked after. I hate to think you're exhausted because of me.'

'Mmm, that's nice—keep doing it and I'll forgive you anything,' she murmured, but Mac had remembered what he *had* said earlier. The problem with not being able to remember exactly what stage their relationship had reached prior to his accident meant he had to move forward with extreme caution. What if they'd discussed living together and she'd said no? Would bringing it up again now only aggravate her?

He moved his fingers lower, digging them in on either side of her spine and relishing her little sighs of pleasure. She did so much for him, it was nice to be able to offer even this small gift of pleasure.

Then suddenly she straightened, moving away so she could turn to face him.

'You were talking about maintaining two establishments,' she said, and it seemed to him her dark eyes looked fearful.

But what could Peterson fear?

No matter what, he reached out, wanting to hold her and promise her he'd protect her from whatever it was, but, as if sensing his reaction, she stood up and shifted to one of the lounge chairs.

'Mac, we have to talk,' she said, the oh, so kissable lips tight with strain. 'I know things have been good between us since you've been living here—apart from when you revert to form and start ordering me around. It's been wonderful and I've enjoyed it, but it's all a lie, Mac.'

Her voice tailed off to a whisper, but that didn't stop the power of the quiet words. They flew like barbed arrows through his skin, sticking in his gut, and lungs and heart.

'The baby's a lie?' he asked, and heard the panic he was feeling in the hoarseness of his voice.

She shook her head impatiently.

'No, the baby's not a lie—it's about the only real thing there is—but, Mac, that's all there was. One night, when we'd both had too much to drink and fell into bed together.' She looked him in the eye, as if daring him to argue, and added, 'It was great. I think we both enjoyed it. But there was no affair—no relationship. In fact, nothing after it.'

He tried to speak, to find words to demand an explanation, but she held up her hand and continued.

'I knew when you talked about amnesia that you assumed we were having a relationship and had forgotten bits of it, and I started to explain to you about what really had happened, but you kissed me and, well, you know what usually happens after that...'

'You're saying all this has been a lie?' The words exploded out of him. 'There *was* no relationship? The night we had dinner with Helene? That was it?'

Peterson nodded, and it seemed to Mac she was diminishing before his eyes, curling herself into the little bug he sometimes called her, but he couldn't stop his own churning emotions escaping in words.

'You let me think I'd forgotten—that I was suffering amnesia—and all this time there was nothing going on between us?'

'I'm sorry,' she whispered, then she straightened up, gathered her hair into a long swatch and with a twitch of her fingers tied it into a knot. It was a movement that always fascinated him as he was certain it defied gravity—though not his questing fingers.

'Actually, I'm not all that sorry.' More certain now, she amended her previous statement. 'You definitely needed someone to keep an eye on you and I was available and, as far as I'm concerned, these last few weeks have been wonderful.'

The defiant glare he associated with Peterson was now firmly back in place, but while she might have recovered from whatever had upset her, he was still lost in a very unpleasant place.

'Are you saying they're over? Thanks for the memory, Mac, now here's your hat and what's your hurry?'

Amelia almost smiled at the silly expression, but it would have been a dim effort at best. Her heart ached with the knowledge that the relationship they'd enjoyed had been based if not on a lie at least on the deception of nondisclosure.

'I'm saying we need to talk about things—to decide about the future.'

Mac frowned at her.

'But there's nothing to decide, woman. We've been

over this before. We're having a baby, and *I'd* rather we were married before it came along. I know some women prefer to wait until after so they'll fit into a sexier dress, but let me tell you this, Peterson, you'll always be sexy to me, dressed or undressed.'

His lips slid into a quirky smile. 'Definitely undressed—now, haven't you been in that daggy uniform long enough?'

Amelia ignored the invitation—and the riffles of excitement his suggestion caused within her—because right now they were back to where they'd been when she'd first told him she was pregnant. Back when he'd assured her that sex and a baby were all he wanted from a marriage.

So nothing had changed—except she'd been foolish enough to fall in love with him.

She studied him, wondering why and how this had happened, and saw a frown gather his eyebrows.

'Well, if you're not going to get undressed, what about the wedding?' he demanded. 'Before or after the baby's born?'

'Are you asking me to marry you?'

Amelia wasn't certain why she was pushing him—because she sure as hell didn't know what she'd reply if he *did* propose.

'Well, not in so many words, Peterson,' he said. 'I mean, it wasn't a formal declaration or anything. Not really a proposal.'

Boy, if he backed away any faster he'd fall over!

'But whether we had a relationship or not before, we've got something going for us now, and we're having a baby together so surely marriage is the answer,' he finished.

Back to the baby, Amelia thought bleakly, but Mac's

assumption that marriage was a foregone conclusion both aggravated and intrigued her.

'And how is this supposed to happen if one or other of us doesn't propose, then go ahead with all the stuff like organising a wedding?' She hesitated, then added, 'And if you say that's women's business, I will throw this chair at you.'

Mac stared at her. She certainly looked angry enough to have the strength to lift the chair and hurl it in his direction. But how had the conversation deteriorated to this? Only minutes ago he'd been massaging her neck and shoulders and her little murmurs of encouragement had led him to believe... In fact, he'd actually been thinking in terms of more massage, but this time as she showered off the weariness of the day. And from massage to...

He fought the lust rising in his blood, and studied the slim, elfin beauty who was the object of that lust. She was angry, no doubt about it, but why?

Because he'd mentioned marriage?

But hadn't he said that all along?

Was it the way he'd talked about it that had upset her?

Should he have proposed in some formal, bended-knee-type way?

'Damn it all, Peterson, you must know I'm not good at this romantic stuff, but if a formal proposal is what you want, then I'll do it. Here? Now?'

It was obvious from her blank-eyed stare that he wasn't doing too well.

He tried again. 'No, I know, we'll go to Capriccio's, where it all started. Saturday night. I'll do it there.'

He beamed at her, sure the brilliance of this idea would bring back the sparkle to her eyes and that seductive smile, which she knew inflamed him, to her lips.

Actually, the spark in her eyes looked more like loathing, and the thin line of her lips suggested more disbelief than seduction.

'Very original choice!' she snapped. 'Makes it easy, does it, to take all your women to the same place?'

She stood up and whirled past him.

'I'm going to have a shower, and then I'm going to bed.' She threw the words at him, turning back to add with unmistakable emphasis, 'Alone.'

Mac stared at the emptiness where she had been—an emptiness echoed in his heart.

He dropped his head into his hands, and reminded himself that every man he'd ever known eventually had to admit he didn't understand women, but sometimes, it seemed to Mac, he had far less understanding than the rest of his gender.

And what had she meant by 'all his women'?

'Do you understand her?' he asked Carl, encountering him in the lift on his way to work the next morning.

'The Bug? She's just a woman,' Carl said. 'And like all of them, there's no telling what'll set her off. But at least with her, she'll soon tell you if she's upset over something. She's never been one to brood or sulk or carry grudges.'

Mac found this heartening. She'd been asleep—or pretending sleep—when he'd looked into the bedroom after a cold and lonely night in the spare bed. And the sight of her, almost childlike in the innocent way she'd lain there, had caught at him—as if his heart had been snagged by a fish hook.

'What were you talking about when she flipped?' Carl asked. He'd established Mac intended getting a cab to work and had offered to drive him, and they were now edging forward through the early morning traffic.

'Dinner at Capriccio's on Saturday night,' Mac replied. 'I thought, as we'd had our first date there, it would be the ideal place to propose.'

Carl turned towards him, his face a study in disbelief.

'And that upset her? Honestly! Women! I doubt there's a man alive who understands them.'

He shook his head, and with the comfort of mutual bewilderment they continued the journey, talking football now, which was far easier to understand.

But as Mac walked into A and E, his thoughts returned to the taut-faced woman who'd sat opposite him the previous evening. She'd definitely been upset, and he'd failed to grasp just why. Had it been because they *hadn't* been having an ongoing affair prior to his accident?

Or because she hadn't told him that was the case?

And either way, surely it didn't matter now. They were having a baby, he enjoyed being with her, was crazy with lust for her delectable body—what more did they need to make a future together?

He greeted colleagues as he made his way—absent-mindedly—to his office.

She was due at work at twelve-thirty. He'd get some flowers and put them on the desk in the little cubby-hole behind the admissions office. Maybe he'd even write a note. Yes, he'd write a note—formally inviting her to dinner.

Should he get a ring?

But if he did and she didn't like it, what would happen?

Would she say so? Or wear a ring she hated for the rest of his life?

He was groaning at the impossibility of it all when Colleen knocked and entered.

'Your head's bad!' she said accusingly, and Mac looked up and frowned his confusion at her.

'My head's fine,' he snapped. 'What do you want?'

Colleen looked as if she'd like to turn around and go right back out again, but she was made of sterner stuff.

'Your concussion was obviously worse than Doug Blake thought,' she said. 'It's morning, and at this time every morning I come in and you fire orders at me, usually rant and rave a little about whatever happens to be upsetting you, then I go back out and try to get as much done as possible before you descend on me with new—and often conflicting—orders.'

She folded her arms and her eyes dared him to argue.

'Am I really that bad?' he asked, and saw her expression change from belligerence to concern.

'*Are* you OK, Mac?' she asked, stepping forward as if she might judge his health better if she was closer.

'Of course I'm OK,' he growled. 'Physically, that is. The rest of me's a mess. Honestly, Colleen, you wouldn't believe the confusion a tiny slip of a thing like Peterson is causing in my life.'

He looked at his secretary and sighed, then added 'Women!' in a tone that consigned them all to perdition.

'I'm a woman,' Colleen reminded him. 'And fast losing patience with this nonsense of yours. If you don't have any correspondence or orders for me, I'll get out of here. And as for Peterson, if you had one iota of sense, you'd be down on your bended knees at least once an hour, giving thanks that such a good, kind, sensible young woman would even give you a second glance—let alone tie herself to you for life.'

She hesitated, then added, 'You *are* going to marry her, I assume?' Her voice boded ill for him if he considered any alternative.

'Of course I'm going to marry her,' he grumbled, then remembered that this hadn't quite been established.

'That's if I can ever sort out what *she* wants for the future.'

He was about to moan 'Women' again in a tone of heartfelt anguish when he remembered Colleen's reaction to his last use of the word.

'What's in the mail?' he said instead, nodding to the pile she still held clutched in one hand.

'Usual government bumf, but there's a letter from your ex about the new trauma centre and a reminder about the meeting of the Lakelands disaster planning committee next Monday night. You've got the MAC meeting Tuesday night and the medical specialists meeting Thursday, so don't plan on much social life next week.'

'I'll write it in my diary—don't get married next week,' Mac said bitterly, then he reached out his hand for the sheaf of papers and got down to work.

The day didn't improve. The vague headache which was the lingering after-effect of his accident worsened as the morning wore on, and by mid-afternoon, when he trapped Peterson in the corridor and invited her to have a coffee with him—something which had become a very pleasant habit lately—she eyed him for a moment, then said 'Your head's aching' in such accusatory tones he snapped at her.

'You don't have to tell me, I already know!'

She accepted his bad-tempered reply with a long-suffering look that tried his patience even further, then demanded to know if he'd spoken to Doug Blake about another scan.

'No, I haven't. Have you spoken to an O and G specialist?'

She blinked her surprise, then coloured in the delicious way she had, making him forget he was angry with her.

Until she answered.

'No, and I don't intend to. Not yet.'

Fear made him grasp her arm and drag her into the tearoom which—just when he needed it—was crowded with people. So he herded her out again, this time pulling open the door to a supply room—fortunately empty.

'You don't mean you're thinking of not having the baby?'

She did the 'startled doe' look females seemed to manage so well, and pulled away from him.

'Of course I intend having the baby,' she shot at him. 'There's just no need to see a specialist this early.'

He thought he was back in the clear, until she added 'Men!' in such scathing tones he actually flinched—then she walked out. And he hadn't seen her since.

So, here he was, at seven o'clock in the evening, sitting at his desk, paperwork more or less up to date but unable to leave because his uncertainty was so strong it was practically rattling his bones. Yesterday at this time—earlier, in fact—he'd sought out Peterson, said goodbye—his skin warmed, thinking of that very private moment—then headed home—well, he now thought of her place as home, didn't he?

Since then, so much had gone wrong he wasn't sure he'd be welcome there, but the thought of returning to his townhouse made his head ache even more.

Well, at least he could do something about the headache. He opened the top drawer of his desk, relaxing slightly and even smiling to himself as he remembered searching for paracetamol during that fateful telephone conversation with Helene.

Pulled out not the blister pack but an envelope. It had arrived the previous day and, aware Colleen had been curious about it—she'd noticed the strongly printed

'Personal' in the corner and had refrained from opening it—he'd shoved it straight into the drawer.

He held it to the light, although he knew who it was from and, after going to his townhouse for clothes and seeing the photo on his dressing-table, could guess what it contained. This must be phase ten—or maybe it was twelve—of Jessica's determination to marry a doctor.

He shook his head as he picked up a paper-knife and slit the envelope open. Did her pursuit of him amount to stalking? Even if it was, could he ever bring himself to report her to the police?

And if he did, what could he say?

A couple of years ago I gave the woman a key to my townhouse so she could let the carpet-cleaners in, and, although she gave it back, she must have had a copy cut because since then she comes and goes at will, leaving cakes or cookies—that was phase one—flowers—that was four or five—and now photos of herself.

He slid the papers from the envelope and unwrapped the photo, turned it over and read the writing on the back.

'All my love, Jessica.'

He studied the woman's fair beauty, thinking how happy it would make him to receive a similar offering from a certain dark-haired nurse.

The thought jolted him so much his fingers clenched, crumpling the shiny paper.

You want Peterson to love you?

Love?

Peterson?

As if summoned by his thoughts, she burst through the door like she always had in the past, the light of battle in her eyes.

'Why are you still here? Is it your head? Did you talk to Doug? Honestly, Mac, you're more trouble than a two-year-old. You know you're supposed to be taking things easy and here you are, working fifteen-hour days. You worried about how the place managed when you were off sick for a fortnight—how do you imagine it'll cope if you keel over with a stroke?'

'Head injuries don't lead to strokes,' he told her, and was pretty sure it was true, but as ever his thinking ability had been undermined by her presence, or by the effect her presence had on the rest of him.

'I don't care what head injuries lead to,' she yelled at him. 'The point is, you shouldn't be here. I've phoned Carl and he's coming to drive you home. And in case you want to argue, I've told him to bring Rob for extra muscle.'

Furious with her attitude, he was about to tell her he could look after himself and certainly didn't need her brothers to ferry him around when he realised that her choice of chauffeurs undoubtedly meant he was to be driven home to her place, not his gloomy townhouse with his irritating neighbour.

His anger disappeared as quickly as it had flared, and he smiled at the still scowling Peterson.

'You'll spoil me with all this attention,' he said, and enjoyed watching her fury change to uncertainty, then her eyes narrow as she tried to work out if he had an ulterior motive in agreeing.

Which he did, of course, and it had a lot to do with where he intended sleeping that night.

'Thank you,' he added, to make her feel even worse, then, because he didn't like to see her frowning, even with uncertainty, he stood up and walked around the desk, taking her in his arms and holding her close while he looked down into her eyes.

'I mean that, Amelia,' he murmured, enjoying the way

the unfamiliar name rolled off his tongue. 'Thank you for everything.'

Then he confirmed the words with a kiss, soon losing himself in her sweetness yet again, so when she pushed away with a breathless 'That's me they're paging' it took him a minute or two to get his bearings.

CHAPTER ELEVEN

AMELIA hurried to answer the call, but her mind was in turmoil. When she'd learned Mac was still at work, concern for him had made her forget their estrangement of the night before and all she'd thought about had been getting him home. Knowing her brothers were working on a building not far from the hospital, and, as the men in charge of the project, they were sure to still be on site, she'd rung Carl and arranged for him to collect Mac from the hospital.

Then, when she'd charged into his office to tell him this and had seen his pale, tired face, all the love she felt for him had welled up and spilled into anger, making her yell when she should have offered comfort. But when that first relieving anger had been spent, she'd noticed what he held in his hands. A photo! And even from the other side of the desk, she'd known damn well it was of Jessica.

Despair so deep it made her guts ache had seized hold of her, and she'd been battling tears when Mac had come around the desk and taken her in his arms. Then he'd kissed her with such sweetness she was sure her heart would break.

Feeble-willed where he was concerned, she'd even kissed him back, and it was lucky she'd been paged, or who knew what might have happened...

All this tumbled through Amelia's mind as she made her way to the emergency entrance. Someone, she couldn't have said who, filled her in—an ambulance arriving with three teenagers, all suffering knife wounds.

Her patient was a teenage girl, bleeding freely but also cursing so fluently whenever her mask was removed that Amelia guessed she wasn't seriously injured.

As the doctor, an intern known to one and all as Rabbit, examined the girl, Amelia began to clean away the blood, coming mainly from a long slash down one arm.

'Wrap that until we can suture it,' Rabbit said. 'I need to check there are no other deep wounds that need more immediate attention.' He was inserting a catheter to take blood then give the patient fluid to replace what she was losing.

Amelia put fresh dressings on the arm, noting but not commenting on the ridged scars indicative of drug abuse, then explained to the girl that the doctor would need to examine her.

'It's easier if I undress you and put you in a hospital gown,' she finished, and copped a mouthful of abuse and a warning not to touch her clothes.

'He stuck me in the arm, nowhere else,' she said with a few colourful expletives thrown in.

Amelia would have liked to have believed her, but it seemed the blood stain on the girl's tiny, tight skirt was growing bigger.

'What about here?' she asked, pressing her gloved hand very gently on the stain.

The girl let out a yell and would have leapt off the bed if Rabbit hadn't been holding her arm.

'Lower right quadrant of the abdomen,' Amelia told the doctor, and as Rabbit shifted so he could lift the short skirt to examine the wound, all hell broke loose.

It was the angry roar that alerted Amelia to trouble, but not soon enough. A knife blade sliced through the curtain, then a leather-clad colossus followed it.

'You hurt my girl—I heard her cry!'

Even with shaggy hair concealing nearly all his face, the pinpoint pupils of his eyes were still visible. The knife-wielder was drugged out of his mind.

He reached out and hauled the young girl off the gurney, ignoring her cries as the catheter was wrenched from her arm and the oxygen mask tangled in her hair.

'Who hurt you?' he demanded, shaking her so violently her head jerked back and forth. Amelia saw the girl's lips move as she tried to answer, then she slumped into a merciful faint.

The action took the giant by surprise and she slipped to the ground, leaving him staring bemusedly at her.

Amelia rushed to her side and with Rabbit's help lifted her back on the gurney. Beyond the torn curtain she knew security people would be gathering and soon the big man would be led away, but all her attention was on the young woman and her condition.

'There'll be internal bleeding—she's better off in Theatre right away,' Rabbit muttered at Amelia as he lifted the girl's skirt and saw the bruised blue edges of the knife wound in the girl's lower abdomen. Amelia was replacing the oxygen mask, while Rabbit found another vein, when the security men appeared.

The big man, who had appeared stunned into immobility, came immediately back to life, grabbing Amelia, who was closest, and holding her against his chest, the deadly, long-handled knife held against her throat.

The three security men stopped moving, though one of them spoke calmly to the man, asking him to release the nurse, explaining she was needed to help the patient.

'She was all right when she came in here—bit of blood in her arm, that's all,' he said.

Amelia, clasped against him, felt curiously detached, as

if it was all happening to someone else. Though the rank smell of the man was real enough.

'I want her better and I want her back now,' he growled.

'She's badly injured—bleeding from a knife wound in her...' Rabbit hesitated, no doubt wondering how to explain, then settled on, 'Stomach.'

'That bastard did that to her! I got him, I know I did. They put him in the ambulance with her.' The string of expletives came out in a howl of rage and pain. 'Where is he? Let me at him!'

He dragged Amelia backwards through the curtains and she caught a glimpse of both her brothers backed up against a wall, held back, no doubt, by the security man in front of them. But nowhere among the faces could she see Mac, though Rick Stewart, senior doctor on duty on the night shift this week, was standing at the end of the row of cubicles, his face white with strain.

'The man you want is in this cubicle,' he called to the man. 'Let the nurse go and the security men will let you in to see him.'

'You can't trap me like that,' the man roared. 'Open up those curtains—let me see the bastard.'

Amelia held her breath. There was no way any doctor would let this madman near a patient, yet Rick had moved towards the curtains—was pulling them open. And there was certainly someone on the gurney, though with the oxygen mask covering his face, and a blood-stained sheet over most of his body, the person was unrecognisable.

Or was he?

'Let the nurse go,' Rick repeated, and Amelia felt the knife move away from her neck, although the man's left arm kept her clamped against his body. Something in the way he moved gave her a clearer view of dark hair and long-lashed eyelids, and recognition slammed through her.

'Mac!' she screamed despairingly, knowing the man with the knife intended to kill him.

'Here she is!' the intruder cried, and, turning, flung her against the two security men. She felt something jab into her side, saw the patient on the gurney move as if to escape the huge man's rage, then, just as she lost consciousness, she cried out again for Mac—certain the knife-wielding madman was about to kill him.

Her body ached all over and her bewildered mind wondered if she might be sick, or if maybe this was how pregnancy felt.

'Amelia? Bug? Little Bug, can you hear me?'

Mac's voice was calling from a long way off. Was the darkness in which she struggled a tunnel of some kind, and he was down the other end?

'Come on, Peterson, you can do better than this! You're in Recovery after surgery and they won't let you out of here until you respond to a voice.'

Ah, that was more like Mac—calling her Peterson, giving orders.

She grasped the hand that was holding hers, hoping it would drag her out of the darkness, and felt a warm pressure in return.

Another hand stroked her forehead, and Mac's voice was coming closer, pleading, cajoling, insisting she respond.

'Mac? You're alive.'

'Of course I'm alive. Someone has to stick around to take care of you,' he growled, and she realised he must be very tired because his voice sounded ragged and hoarse. Then she remembered he'd been ill and shouldn't be getting tired.

'You should be home in bed,' she told him, and hoped he understood because the words sounded very jumbled to her. 'It's so dark it must be late.'

'Open your eyes and look at me,' he said. 'It's not so dark, Amelia.'

It was so strange to hear Mac calling her Amelia, she did open her eyes—or at least she tried, but her eyelids weighed about a ton and she rather thought her eyelashes might be stuck together.

'For me, Little Bug—just open them for me?'

He sounded so gently persuasive she tried again, and this time Mac's face swam into focus.

Mac's exhausted face!

She tried to scold him but it was too hard to make the words, so instead she held his hands and went to sleep.

Her mother was beside her next time she woke, and the anxiety in the brown eyes made Amelia look around.

'I'm in hospital?' she said, trying to sit up then deciding it hurt too much and staying prone. 'Why? What happened? Was it the same accident when Mac was hurt? How can we both be in hospital? Who will look after him?'

But even as she asked the questions, memory came flooding back.

'The man with the knife. My side hurt. Did he stab me?'

Her mother nodded, tears brimming in her eyes.

'Yes, darling, quite badly. I don't know all the technical terms, but apparently the knife perforated your intestine and also cut a blood vessel. You lost a lot of blood, and they had to operate to fix things up inside you.'

Her mother wasn't crying because she'd been hurt,

Amelia realised. Something else bad had happened. Her hand crept to her abdomen and she pressed it there.

'The baby?'

More tears streaked down her mother's face as she confirmed Amelia's worst fears with a single nod.

'I'm sorry, darling. The surgeons think it was the blood you lost that caused the miscarriage. There was no damage to your body—to that part of your body. You can have other babies.'

But not Mac's babies, Amelia thought, and felt dampness on her cheeks as the agony in her broken heart spilled over.

She must have slept for when she woke her mother was gone and a nurse she didn't know was fussing over her.

'Your family has all been in—boy, are those brothers of yours good-looking—but you keep sleeping through their visits. And we're all under orders from that ogre downstairs in A and E to contact him the moment you wake up. He sat by your bed all through the first night and only Doug Blake telling him he'd drop dead if he didn't rest stopped him staying last night.'

'Last night? What time is it? And how long have I been here?'

'Two days here—and a night in Theatre and Recovery so today's the third day since it happened.'

Amelia tried to work out where the days had gone, and what, if anything, she remembered of them.

'My mother was here?'

The nurse nodded.

'Yesterday morning—well, she's been here more than that, but you woke up and talked to her yesterday.'

Treacherous tears threatened to escape again when Amelia recalled, in all too vivid detail, her mother's visit, but she fought them back. Apparently, she'd escaped into the nether world of sleep to blot the pain from her mind, but she couldn't stay asleep for ever. She had to face not only the fact that she'd lost the baby but that she'd lost Mac as well.

All too easily she recalled the look on his face when she'd barged into his office to tell him to go home and had found him holding the picture of Jessica. The look of longing in his eyes had been unmistakable.

Well, now he was free to return to his beautiful blonde.

'I'm sure they need nurses in Siberia,' Amelia muttered to herself, though she doubted even there would be far enough away for her to forget Mac—forget the way he held her in his arms, stroked his fingers through her hair, called her Little Bug...

She drew in a deep breath and told herself she had to start as she meant to go on. The nurse had disappeared and was probably phoning Mac right now. Providing there was no emergency downstairs, he'd be on his way up before she knew it.

She lifted the phone beside the bed and dialled the nurses' station. She might not have been a patient before, but she'd worked the wards long enough to know how the phone system worked.

'This is Amelia Peterson. I just wanted to ask if you could restrict all visitors to my immediate family—that's four brothers and my parents—and no one else.'

Her voice sounded so weak and wavery she doubted they'd argue, but even as she hung up she heard Mac's voice outside.

'Of course she doesn't mean me,' he declared. 'We're engaged, about to be married.'

A pause, which gave time for Amelia to get over the shock of that statement, then, 'She was at work when it happened—how many nurses do you know wear their engagement rings to work? This is ridiculous, and anyway I'm senior to you and I'm going in.'

Amelia almost smiled as she imagined some poor nurse backing away from Mac's temper, then the door opened and he was there.

'Some stupid nurse tried to stop me seeing you,' he told her, striding across the room and stopping by the bed, looking down at her with a frown that should have stopped the nurse arguing right from the start. 'You're still far too pale. What's that surgeon giving you? Plasma, by the look of it—I wonder if it should be full blood.'

For a moment Amelia thought he'd march right out again, no doubt to give orders to the surgeon, but instead he checked her chart, studied her again, then slumped down in the chair beside the bed.

Amelia watched him warily. So far, he'd been 'Mac the head of A and E', treating her as he would any of his staff in her situation. There was no sign of Mac the lover, and though she knew she should be relieved, her heart grieved that she'd already lost him.

An eternity—that was possibly only seconds—later, he reached out and took her hand.

'Your mother told you about the baby?'

Half-statement, half-question.

Amelia nodded.

'I'm sorry, Peterson,' he said, lifting her hand and pressing it against his cheek. 'It was the sort of stupid accident that should never have happened, and for it to happen to you...'

His head lifted and she read the anguish in his eyes, and knew it was for the child he really had wanted.

The love she felt for him meant she had to offer comfort, even when her entire body was aching with the double loss.

'It'll be OK,' she said softly. 'And at least it leaves you free now, not tied to someone you don't love because of the baby. You'll have other children—you and Jessica.'

His hand gripped hers so hard she flinched, but even as he echoed the woman's name his pager buzzed, and with a furious scowl he pulled it from his pocket, read the message, swore and stood up.

'Jessica?' he repeated. 'The witch who lives next door to me? How on earth did you get it into your stupid head, Peterson, that I might ever, even in my wildest dreams, want anything to do with that rapacious woman?'

His voice had risen to a dull roar, bringing a nurse hurrying into the room.

'No wonder you didn't want him visiting,' she said, and Mac turned his fury on her.

'Did she say that? Say she didn't want me visiting? Mention me by name?'

The nurse backed down, shaking her head but bravely remaining in the room. The pager buzzed again, and Mac stormed out, pausing in the doorway to turn back to Amelia.

'I'll be back,' he said, sounding so threatening that if Amelia hadn't known him she'd have booked herself out of hospital immediately.

As it was, she had plenty to think about. Mac's reaction to Jessica's name had been genuine.

But even if he didn't love the blonde beauty, he didn't love her, Amelia, either, and, loving him as she did, she didn't think she could live with him and hide it.

He did come back, but not until evening when Rob and her father were visiting. Amelia listened to her father and brother's conversation, but was aware of Mac's impatience to be alone with her. He was practically twitching with it.

It was only so he could finish his argument, she knew, but her silly heart wanted to believe he was eager just to be with her.

In the end he cracked and, grasping an elbow each of her brother and her father, all but hoisted them out of the visitors' chairs.

'Rob, Alec, I know you've both been worried to death about her—hell's teeth, we all have—but right now if I don't have some time alone with her, to ram a few truths into her foolish head, I'll go mad.'

Her father looked amused, but Rob, always her defender, took offence at Mac's tone.

'We'll only leave if she asks us to go,' he said, then he turned to Amelia. 'You want us out of here, Bug?'

Amelia shrugged, then said, 'Not really, but I've seen him lose his temper with bigger people than you, so maybe you'd better go and let him have his say.'

They both bent and kissed her cheek, then left, though Amelia suspected Rob would hover outside the door, ready to return if she needed him.

Mac shut the door, then came over to the bed, running his fingers through his hair and looking as confused as she'd ever seen him.

'I haven't a clue where to begin, Peterson,' he said. 'You've got me so tied up in knots I don't know which way's up.'

He slumped into the chair and reached out to take her hand, clutching it as if it might lead him out of his confusion.

'Jessica—I'll start there, though how you ever got the stupid idea I might be interested in her I'll never know!'

He frowned to impress her stupidity on her, but Amelia wasn't worried by his frowns. She was holding her breath, wondering just what was to come—wondering if, by some miraculous chance, Mac's confusion might be connected to her, to the way he felt about her...

'I moved into that townhouse after the divorce—it's all I got out of it, and when the tenants left I thought I might as well use the darned place. Jessica lived next door then, and right from the start she showed she was interested in me. As you can imagine, Peterson, a woman was the last thing I needed in my life.'

Amelia's heart sank at the switch back to being 'Peterson', and a little further with the final phrase, but she had no time to brood over her reaction as he was talking again.

'She had a key and did the cake and biscuit thing, and I thought she was being neighbourly, but it went too far. She's stalking me, Peterson.'

Amelia would have laughed at the outrage in his voice if she wasn't still his old colleague Peterson, not his love Amelia or even Little Bug!

'She left flowers, meals, presents, then lately she started leaving photos. You probably saw one in the bedroom that she must have sneaked in when I was in hospital, and she sent another one last week. The woman's mad, but I think she's harmless—well, I thought she was until you got it into your thick head I had some kind of interest in her.'

He glared at Amelia as if expecting some reply to what he saw as treachery on her part, but she was telling her over-excited heart that Mac not being in love with Jessica was one thing, but didn't automatically mean he might be even slightly in love with anyone else—namely one Amelia Peterson!

'Well, haven't you anything to say for yourself?' he demanded.

Amelia shrugged and tried for total cool.

'It's actually none of my business whether you're interested in her or not.'

Her voice wavered so much she missed cool by a mile, then she remembered something else.

'And what about the dinner at Capriccio's? The receipt was dated only a few days after you'd asked me to be your occasional lover. If you didn't take Jessica to dinner there, who did you take? It certainly wasn't me!'

She folded her arms across her chest and glared at him—knowing she'd caught him now.

He was frowning as if he had no idea what Capriccio's was, let alone who he might have taken there, then his brow cleared and he laughed, the sound so joyous and familiar Amelia's heart jolted with the pain of loving him.

'Going through my pockets, were you?'

'I was not,' Amelia objected huffily. 'You gave me the receipt—you wrote your phone numbers on it. Dinner for two!'

Mac continued to smile.

'I can even tell you the date,' he said. 'It was the last MAC meeting I attended. I took Enid Biggs to dinner to talk her into agreeing with your in-service training idea.'

Now he folded his arms, leaning back in the chair with self-righteous satisfaction. But it wasn't his look that affected Amelia—more the content of his words.

'You took Enid Biggs out to dinner?'

He nodded, looking almost smug.

'For me?'

Another nod, then his innate honesty must have prompted him to add, 'Well, I could see the benefit to the department, and with the possibility of St Pat's getting the major trauma centre...'

He left the sentence unfinished, and edged the chair nearer the bed.

'Now, is there anything else you want to yell at me about, or do you think maybe I could kiss you?'

Amelia looked into the deep-set eyes, and saw the softness she'd seen as they'd made love. Her insides liquefied, and all she wanted to do was reach out and take him in her arms—to hold him and be held by him.

For ever!

But there was more at stake than her feelings and emotions. Mac had reacted well to her pregnancy, but to tie him to her now would be unfair.

Was she strong enough to let him go?

Strong enough to pretend it was what she wanted?

She took her lead from him, and faced him as she had so often—as a colleague, not a lover.

'I have not yelled at all,' she said, summoning every drop of dignity she possessed. 'In fact, yelling would probably hurt my stitches, but the fact remains, Mac, that we're no longer tied by a pregnancy, and though you were absolutely wonderful…' Her voice was breaking up but she hoped he'd put that down to hoarseness from the tube she'd had down her throat during and just after the operation. 'There's no need for you to feel obliged to stick around. We're both free to go our own way now, which is really good, don't you think?'

She finally wavered to a halt and looked anxiously into his face, trying to read a response.

'No!' he said, though his face remained impassive.

'What do you mean, no?'

'No, I don't think it's really good,' he elaborated. 'And I'm going to put it down to the fact that you're still far from well, because that's the only explanation I can find for you to be talking such utter nonsense.'

He reached out and took her hand again, and leaned forward so his face was only inches from hers.

'When that madman had you in his arms, Peterson, I thought my world was coming to an end. I realised that without you life wouldn't be worth living.'

He leaned forward a little more and threaded his fingers into her hair.

'Amelia? Little Bug? You know me well enough to know I can't do flowery speeches and that I'm more likely to yell at you than pay you pretty compliments, but you've become dearer to me than life itself, closer to my heart than I could ever imagine, more important to me than my work, or my health, or anything I can think of.'

Amelia heard the words but, more, she heard the truth in his voice, and her heart thudded with a hope too overwhelming to put into words.

'It's your turn to say something,' he said, the huskiness in his voice vibrating along her nerves. 'I know you're still weak from what's happened, but it's only one word, Amelia. One little ''yes'', that's all I want from you.'

Amelia did a mental replay of words already engraved in her mind.

'Yes?' she queried. 'But you didn't ask me anything.'

Mac frowned.

'Of course I did. I asked you to marry me, surely you worked that out.'

He sounded so put out Amelia had to smile, then she reached up and rested her hand against his cheek.

'What about love?' she asked. 'You haven't mentioned that.'

'I must have—weren't you listening? Love's all part of it, Amelia. That's what's rocked me so much. To think that after wasting all this time, I'd fall in love with a little snip of a thing who's been right under my nose for years. Of course I love you. Now it's your turn again. And not to argue, just to say you love me, too, and, yes, you'd love to marry me.'

He looked so anxious Amelia drew his head down towards her and kissed him softly on the lips.

'Yes, Mac, I love you, too, and I'd love to marry you.'

She kissed him again, then released him, pushing him far enough back she could look into his eyes.

'That's if you ask me properly.'

Mac growled, but in the end he did ask properly, kneeling by the hospital bed, Amelia's hand clasped against his chest so she could feel the thudding of his heart as it beat a rhythm so in tune with hers she knew this love would last for ever.

EPILOGUE

FIFTEEN months later, Amelia was in hospital again, although this time in a different ward. Her room was awash with flowers, though very few of them were visible, the bed being surrounded by a surfeit of grumbling visitors.

'It's not that we're not pleased to see you, Bug,' Alistair was saying earnestly, while Carl and Rowley chatted to Mac's parents, 'but we can see *you* anytime. We really came to see the baby. There we all stood, like big galoots, peering in through the glass window of the nursery, admiring every baby wrapped in a blue blanket. It wasn't until Mum and Dad arrived, and Mum cast her grandmotherly eye over all the babies available for inspection and shook her head, that we realised he wasn't there.'

'Apparently Mac arrived just before us,' Carl explained, turning towards the bed, 'and whisked his son away.'

'Well, they won't have gone far,' Amelia said, moving over in the bed to make room for her mother to perch on one side.

'No?' Alec McDougal said, cocking an eyebrow in Amelia's direction. 'When Petra was born, he carried her around half the hospital, introducing her to all the staff on duty, from the lowliest porter to the Medical Superintendent or whoever it is runs the place.'

'And that was just his niece,' Marion McDougal added. 'Think how much prouder he'd be of his own son.'

Amelia chuckled, but had to acknowledge Mac's parents were right. If people could actually burst with pride, it was a wonder it hadn't happened to Mac. He'd been with her right through the delivery, though he'd harassed the staff so constantly it was a wonder he'd been allowed to stay, but when the small, slippery baby had been placed in his hands he'd been speechless, simply staring at the red, squalling bundle while tears had slid unchecked down his cheeks. Her beloved ogre reduced to silent wonderment by the miracle of birth.

And though she smiled at the memory, she had to admit it hadn't taken him long to recover, issuing orders about the care of his son to all and sundry.

'It doesn't make you feel redundant, this obsession Mac has with the baby?'

Charlotte, who'd just arrived and been told about the 'Grand Tour,' moved close enough to kiss Amelia's cheek and hand her more flowers.

'Not in the slightest,' Amelia told her honestly, her own eyes growing misty as she remembered the aftermath of the birth, when the baby had been taken away to be washed and dressed, and she and Mac had finally had some time alone.

'What are you going to call him?' Charlotte asked. 'Mac said you still hadn't decided.'

'Yes, we have.'

Mac answered as he walked in, the baby looking even tinier when tucked against his tall frame.

'We're calling him Connor.' He smiled across at Amelia, who was so startled by this announcement she could only stare at him. 'So you can all meet him, then I want you out of here. My wife's had a long, hard labour and needs to rest.'

He shot Amelia a look that dared her to argue, but she had no intention of arguing. She loved her family, and had grown close to Mac's as well, but she'd slept for hours after the delivery and so had barely had time to get to know her son—let alone see much of her husband who, at some time between when she'd seen him briefly an hour ago and now, had decided to go along with her choice of a name.

'Why?' she asked, when the visitors had left and Connor was sleeping soundly in a crib by her bed.

'Why Connor?' Mac asked, making himself comfortable on her bed. His back was resting against her pillows, his long legs were stretched out on the bed and one arm held her firmly against his body.

He turned and smiled at her, then brushed a gentle kiss across her lips.

'Because it was the name chosen by the most wonderful woman in the world, that's why. I know I argued and blustered and said it was Irish and didn't go with a Scottish surname, but you must have known, in the end, I'd give in to you. Don't I always?'

He kissed her again, but Amelia wasn't distracted by this tactic, kissing him back then moving away so she could remind him of a couple of dozen times that sprang immediately to mind when he hadn't come even close to giving in to her.

Mac laughed, and hugged her closer.

'But in the important things, we usually agree,' he reminded her.

He traced the contours of her face with his finger.

'Don't we, Little Bug?'

She didn't argue—couldn't—because the love shining in his eyes had taken her breath away and left a lump the size of Ireland in her throat.

'And though I'm proud of Connor, and thrilled to be a father, and really love this family thing, you're still my miracle, Amelia. So much so I sometimes wonder what

I've done to deserve such luck and happiness. In fact...'
he kissed her again as if he needed the contact to sort out
his thoughts '...if I didn't know you'd hate it, I'd carry
you around the hospital the way I carried Connor, just so
everyone could see what a lucky man I am.'

Amelia smiled at him.

'We wouldn't get very far,' she said. 'I reckon before
we were out of the maternity ward you'd be telling me I
should be lying differently, or you'd see a patient you first
met in A and E and would probably forget you were holding me, drop me on the ground and rush over to check
she was being treated properly.'

'Nonsense,' Mac growled, kissing her again. 'I'd at
least set you on your feet.'

LIVE THE EMOTION

Modern Romance™
...seduction and
passion guaranteed

Tender Romance™
...love affairs that
last a lifetime

Medical Romance™
...medical drama
on the pulse

Historical Romance™
...rich, vivid and
passionate

Sensual Romance™
...sassy, sexy and
seductive

Blaze Romance™
...the temperature's
rising

27 new titles every month.

Live the emotion

MILLS & BOON®

MB3

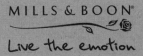

MILLS & BOON®

Live the emotion

Medical Romance™

A VERY SPECIAL MARRIAGE *by Jennifer Taylor*

Nurse Sophie Patterson was looking forward to a fresh start as resident nurse on board a luxury liner bound for the Mediterranean – until she discovered that her boss was Dr Liam Kennedy, her ex-husband! Her desire for him is brought back into stark reality, and Sophie's immediate response is to run. But Liam has realised he'll never love anyone as much as her – can he persuade her to stay…?

THE ELUSIVE CONSULTANT *by Carol Marinelli*

Emergency charge nurse Tessa Hardy is stunned to discover that Max Slater is moving to England – without his fiancée! Tess is secretly in love with Max, though she knows she can't admit her feelings. Yet during a daring rescue operation Max stuns her by passionately kissing her – is this elusive consultant ready to be tamed? (*A&E Drama* miniseries)

ENGLISHMAN AT DINGO CREEK *by Lucy Clark*

Dr Dannyella Thompson certainly needed help in her Outback practice – but an English doctor? She thought he'd be more amusement than assistance. But Dr Sebastian MacKenzie proved her wrong at every turn, and by the time his stay was up he'd won her over – in every way! Except to convince her that she should return to England with him as his bride… (*Doctors Down Under* miniseries)

On sale 5th September 2003

Available at most branches of WHSmith, Tesco, Martins, Borders, Eason, Sainsbury's and all good paperback bookshops.

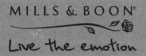

Invitations to Seduction

THREE SIZZLING STORIES FROM TODAY'S HOTTEST WRITERS!

VICKI LEWIS THOMPSON
CARLY PHILLIPS · JANELLE DENISON

Available from 15th August 2003

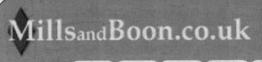

FREE!

4 Books
and a surprise gift!

We would like to take this opportunity to thank you for reading this Mills & Boon® book by offering you the chance to take FOUR more specially selected titles from the Medical Romance™ series absolutely FREE! We're also making this offer to introduce you to the benefits of the Reader Service™—

- ★ FREE home delivery
- ★ FREE gifts and competitions
- ★ FREE monthly Newsletter
- ★ Books available before they're in the shops
- ★ Exclusive Reader Service discount

Accepting these FREE books and gift places you under no obligation to buy; you may cancel at any time, even after receiving your free shipment. Simply complete your details below and return the entire page to the address below. *You don't even need a stamp!*

YES! Please send me 4 free Medical Romance books and a surprise gift. I understand that unless you hear from me, I will receive 6 superb new titles every month for just £2.60 each, postage and packing free. I am under no obligation to purchase any books and may cancel my subscription at any time. The free books and gift will be mine to keep in any case.

M3ZEF

Ms/Mrs/Miss/Mr ....Initials................................
BLOCK CAPITALS PLEASE

Surname..

Address..

....

....Postcode ....

Send this whole page to:
UK: The Reader Service, FREEPOST CN81, Croydon, CR9 3WZ
EIRE: The Reader Service, PO Box 4546, Kilcock, County Kildare (stamp required)

Offer not valid to current Reader Service subscribers to this series. We reserve the right to refuse an application and applicants must be aged 18 years or over. Only one application per household. Terms and prices subject to change without notice. Offer expires 28th November 2003. As a result of this application, you may receive offers from Harlequin Mills & Boon and other carefully selected companies. If you would prefer not to share in this opportunity please write to The Data Manager at the address above.

Mills & Boon® is a registered trademark owned by Harlequin Mills & Boon Limited.
Medical Romance™ is being used as a trademark.